Whispers of Ichicka

Volume 1

GAEA AND CADOR'S FATE

TANYA VAN ASWEGEN

WARNING

Reader discretion is advised. This is a dark fantasy novel and contains scenes of violence that may be unsettling for some readers.

ACKNOWLEDGMENTS

YHWH

Thank you to my mom Jenette, Rudolph, and Rochelle

CONTENTS

PROLOGUE

Ichicka Forest... even the name itself felt ominous, like a story whispered through generations. It held secrets and mysteries as tangled as its roots, and its beauty was unlike any other place on earth. For the Angevins, it was more than just trees and shadows. It was home — a part of us filled with a curious history, ancient pacts, and old magic.

Mamo blessed me with the name Gaea, the meaning of which resembles Mother Nature herself. I've heard stories about the forest calling lost souls to her, and maybe that's why Ichicka always called to me. When I was a child, I'd lose myself in the depths of her greens — listening to the wind sing through the treetops, pretending I was a fairy queen with a crown of wildflowers.

But even as a child, I could feel the old magic stirring beneath the surface — stories whispered in the rustling leaves, unknown to me then, of the sacred pact my family made long ago to protect the balance between our world and the wild.

Mamo and Papo were the only world I knew. Their love was the sun on my face, their laughter the soundtrack to my days. Then, in an instant, they were gone — disappeared without a trace. The forest, once a place of magic and adventure, became a silent ache in my chest, a reminder of everything I'd lost.

Now, nearing my eighteenth birthday, I stand on the edge of a new and terrifying uncertainty. Torn from the farm, the forest, and the secrets they've left behind, everything I thought I knew is unraveling. The weight of prophecy — a destiny I never asked for — presses down on me. New questions rise from old answers never found, pulling me deeper into Ichicka's dark heart.

The whispers grow louder now. The stories are coming alive — not just about my family, or why the forest calls me… but about something deep inside myself. Something that could help me heal. Ichicka has always been there, watching, waiting. And I think, maybe, it holds all the answers I need.

The forest is waking.

The past is stirring.

And so is the prophecy.

CHAPTER ONE

I loved listening to Papo's stories about our family, the Angevins. He said we were one of the first original families in Graceway. He said that one of the greats, Cormac Angevin battled alongside big, mythical creatures against some ancient evil.

"They saved Graceway," he'd say. It was my favorite bedtime story.

"Papo, why can't I go into the forest alone? I won't go in too far, promise. I will stay near the edge."

"I trust you, Love, but we have a few problems with sick animals running around. I do not want you to get hurt, especially when you are alone. It's only to keep you safe."

"But…"

"No buts, Gaea, now sleep there, my angel," Papo said and kissed me on the forehead.

"Night, Papo, love you."

"Love you too."

"You can help me tomorrow morning pick some flowers from the garden. I want to make some soaps for the market." Mamo said as she entered the room

"Oh yes, I would love that, thanks, Mamo. I love you."

"Night, my darling," Mamo said as she switched off the bed light and kissed Gaea goodnight.

I tried to go to sleep but it felt as if something or someone was calling me. Ichicka. I could feel her again—like a shadow brushing the edge of my mind. Calling me.

The cool, damp bark of the trees, the earthy smell of the ground after rain filling my lungs. The soft, green moss under my bare feet growing beneath the ancient oaks. It felt like Grammy's carpet, but alive. And the wind, whispering through the leaves, wasn't just wind. I heard the birds singing in the trees, talking to me.

I didn't want to upset Mamo and Papo. But the truth is, I've gone into the forest many times without them knowing. I hated lying to them... but the forest felt more like home than any house ever could.

I loved being outside, a part of nature, feeling the sun on my skin and the rays highlighting my green eyes. I slowly drifted away as the thoughts of the next day's adventure filled my dreams.

CHAPTER TWO

"*Aaaghh,*" I yawned and stretched widely as I woke up. The soft clattering of pots and pans from the kitchen below told me Mamo was already making breakfast.

I can't wait to get outside in the sun, I thought, hopping out of bed. *But first—shower.*

My closet had two sections: one for folded clothes and one with double doors for hanging them. *I feel like shorts and a T-shirt,* I decided, grabbing a blue top and black shorts before rushing into the bathroom.

The warm water felt like a gentle hug, wrapping around me, tingling all my senses. Mamo's lavender soap filled the air—earthy, clean, and soothing. I pulled my long curly hair into a ponytail, grabbed my toothbrush, and squeezed the minty paste onto the bristles. The sharp scent hit my nose, and the sweet, icy taste jolted my senses awake.

I ran downstairs, energized.

"Oh wow, Mamo, it smells delicious!" I grinned. The rich smell of coffee, salty scrambled eggs, and warm toast made my mouth water.

"I made breakfast before our garden adventure," she said with a smile.

"Where's Papo? He never sleeps late."

"No, Love, he left early this morning. Had to tend to some business with Mayor Stein."

"More eggs for me, then," I giggled, sliding into my chair.

"We also need to pick some oranges today. This is the last of the juice," Mamo said as she handed me a glass.

"Are we going to do something special this weekend, Mamo?"

"Not that I can think of. Why do you ask, Love?"

"Just curious," I said, trying to sound casual. I was turning ten this Friday. Mamo and Papo usually surprised me with something magical.

I was always amazed at how talented Mamo was. She made sourdough bread from scratch, jams from the fruit in our garden, and churned butter from the cream she skimmed off our cows' milk. She even made our soaps, shampoos, toothpaste—everything natural— and sold them at the farmer's market on Saturdays. I was homeschooled and loved our time together.

"When you're done, rinse your plate and juice glass, then meet me outside. I'm going to prepare our baskets and the trolley for our adventure," Mamo said, snapping me out of my thoughts.

She packed a picnic basket with berries, cheese, crackers, juice, and water bottles, then placed everything carefully inside a cooler box fitted snugly into our adventure trolley.

Papo had made the trolley for me. He was a woodworker, and it was one of my favorite things he'd ever built—a lightweight wooden box with a sturdy handle and six all-terrain caster wheels. It could go anywhere.

I rinsed my dishes and burst out the kitchen door, leaping over the three steps.

"TA-DA! What are your next two wishes?" I declared with a flourish.

"Silly girl," Mamo laughed. "Let's get going. I want to be back before your father gets home to prepare dinner."

Mamo's herb and flower garden was stunning. The flowers were thick with scent—sweet and heavy. Bees danced from bloom to bloom, buzzing in rhythm with the warm breeze. We picked lavender, roses, jasmine, lilac, and a few others she used for soaps and medicine. Then we collected fruits—strawberries, blueberries, cherries, plums, and oranges.

"We're done, my Love. You can go and play while I head back, unpack, and start dinner."

"Thanks, Mom!" I said, maybe a little too quickly.

"Not into the forest, Gaea," she warned, eyebrows raised.

"Not into the forest," I repeated, mockingly obedient.

We had newborn lambs and goats on the farm, and I couldn't wait to play with them. I loved watching them jump and frolic. I'd lie in the long grass, giggling as it tickled my fingers, rolling with the lambs.

Sometimes it felt like the grass was trying to make me laugh—like it was playing too.

Today, I won't go into the forest, I promised myself. *I'll just sit near the edge and wait.*

Small animals often came out—rabbits, squirrels, even deer. They'd dart around me, curious, playful. Being an only child, I treasured their company. I'd make up stories and talk to them for hours. It was all I knew. And I loved it.

Mamo came from Wave Crest, a big city two days' drive north of Graceway. She was beautiful, with short golden-blonde hair and light brown streaks that caught the sun. Her eyes were warm and brown, flecked with gold like little sunbeams. She loved deeply, with a heart big enough to hold all of us and still have room for the world. She studied herbalism at Wave Crest University.

Papo was from Graceway. He was tall—giant-like—with broad shoulders and brown curls that brushed his shoulders. His eyes were summer-sky blue, and his skin always looked sun-kissed, like he'd just come from the beach. Loud, funny, and kind, he had a deep love for animals.

They met at Wave Crest University—in the library, of all places. Mamo was a teacher's aide. Papo was still studying. They said it was like lightning struck. They fell in love fast, married after he graduated, and moved to Graceway to the family farm. His parents had passed away when he was in his late teens, leaving it all to him.

Star-crossed lovers, they called themselves. Meant to be. And now here they were—with me—living quietly, in a place where the forest always seemed to be watching.

CHAPTER THREE

The sunlight spilled into my room, painting the pink rumpled sheets in a warm, golden hue. Late summer, early autumn—those mornings were crisp, and the afternoons glowed. I lay sprawled on the bed, my blonde curls a tangled mess, still half-asleep.

Friday morning had finally arrived—**my tenth birthday!** It was the start of the school break, though classes would resume on Monday. Mamo and Papo tried to come in quietly, their soft voices carrying the melody of a birthday song.

My room was tucked into the corner of the house, overlooking the yard all the way to where the trees of Ichicka Forest began. It had warm wooden floors, a large window, and a built-in bench—my favourite place to lose myself in thought. Across the hall was their room, much bigger and always scented with Mamo's lavender oil. Downstairs, the kitchen was enormous. That was where Mamo worked her magic, surrounded by her soaps, medicines, and the ever-present aroma of baking and cooking.

"Happy birthday to you, happy birthday to you..." they sang, their voices warm and close.

"Good morning, Sunshine. Did you sleep well? We have a surprise," Mamo whispered, brushing a soft hand through my hair.

"Not just one surprise," Papo added playfully, sitting on the floor beside my bed.

Mamo kissed my forehead, her lips gentle and warm.

"Mamo! Papo! Cake?" I grinned, my voice still half-asleep.

They laughed, a warm and comforting sound.

"We'll have cake later," Mamo promised, her eyes twinkling. "But first, other surprises."

She placed a present in my lap—wrapped in rough, brown paper and tied with string.

"I made the paper myself," she said, her voice proud.

Inside, I found a backpack and a sleeping bag.

"Wow!" I breathed, my eyes wide with awe.

Papo slid closer with a larger gift in his hands. "This one," he said, "is extra special."

I tore at the paper, my heart pounding.

"No way!" I gasped, jumping out of bed. "A tent! My own tent!" Tears of joy blurred my vision. "Thank you, thank you!"

"And," Mamo added with a mysterious smile, "the best surprise of all... We're camping in Ichicka Forest tonight. Just the three of us."

I threw my arms around them, a happy sob catching in my throat.

"Best birthday ever!" I cried.

"Pancakes for breakfast?" Mamo asked as she and Papo headed downstairs.

I nodded eagerly, already rummaging through my closet for clothes. I grabbed a pair of blue jeans, my "Daddy's Little Angel" T-shirt, socks, and hiking boots, then ran into my ensuite bathroom. The shower felt like warm summer rain, washing away the sleep. I brushed my teeth—too much mint, but I didn't care. I braided my hair, ready for the adventure ahead.

I nearly tripped down the stairs, drawn by the heavenly smell of Mamo's pancakes. *Best smell ever*, I thought, plopping into my chair. Mamo placed the golden stack in front of me, and in the centre of the table stood a jug of freshly squeezed orange juice— made from the fruit we'd picked just days earlier. The sweet scent of syrup, warm batter, and bright citrus filled the room.

I gobbled the pancakes a bit too quickly, my mind already in the forest.

Mamo had packed my things the night before without me noticing—meals, gear, everything. All I had to do was grab them.

"Fetch your new backpack and sleeping bag. Your clothes are on the side table in the living room," Mamo said as she cleared the table. "You can pack everything, and then we'll be on our way."

I did exactly that, and minutes later, we stepped outside, our boots crunching on the gravel path toward the trees.

We hiked for hours, the forest a thick, green, magical world. Birds sang high-pitched melodies, the cool wind whispered through the leaves, and wildflowers filled the air with the scent of honey and cinnamon. Mamo pointed out plants and explained their uses. Papo showed me animal tracks and told me what to look for when tracking them. The forest was their world—and finally, mine too.

We set up camp by a stream that flowed like silver ribbon from somewhere deep in Graceway. The water was cool, clear, and sang as it moved.

"Can I explore?" I begged.

"Yes, but stay nearby," Mamo warned. "This is still the home of wildlife. We're in *their* territory."

"I understand," I nodded, then turned and followed the stream.

I pretended I was a fairy queen, speaking to squirrels and dragonflies, singing to them as if they were my subjects. I stayed close to the stream, careful not to stray too far.

Then—a rustle in the bushes. I froze. The feeling of being watched wrapped around me like a cold fog. I turned and ran back to camp, a shiver crawling up my spine.

Mamo was preparing dinner—hearty beef stew and bread baked right in the fire. I was starving. We sat by the flames and devoured the meal. Afterward, Papo told stories of the forest—of wolves, old pacts, and ancient guardians. He roared like a wolf, and we all laughed until our stomachs hurt.

Mamo pulled out marshmallows, chocolate, and crackers.

"One more thing—we need S'mores before bed."

"Yeah, S'mores!" I sang, bouncing in excitement.

I loved roasting my own marshmallows, though I still needed Papo's help to assemble the perfect S'more. He never minded.

"Bedtime, Sunshine," Mamo said softly. "Big hike back home tomorrow."

"I don't want to go," I whispered, hugging them both. Their love wrapped around me like a warm blanket.

"Thank you for the perfect birthday. I don't think you'll ever top this one," I giggled as I crawled into my new tent.

That night, as I drifted into sleep, a strange dream found me.

A wolf by the stream. Mamo and Papo by the fire, their laughter falling into silence. Their eyes fixed on me—not smiling. A cold wind. The stench of sulfur. The fire snuffed out with a hiss.

I woke with a jolt, my heart racing. The dream clung to me like smoke.

CHAPTER FOUR

Mary-Ann and Peter stayed up late, wrapped in the warm glow of a crackling fire.

"I need to pick yellow sunberry flowers and green-rooted brush on the way home tomorrow," Mary-Ann said with a flicker of frustration. "Maybe I can make a concoction for the poison spreading among the young wolves."

Peter's voice trembled slightly as he replied, "I have a bad feeling about this. I read through Cormac's diary, hoping to find clues about this sickness, but it's not good. It's very similar to what brought him to Ichicka in the first place. This means our baby girl is in serious danger."

Mary-Ann's eyes darkened. "I spoke to Mayor Stein during the week. Only a few of the original families remain, and no one knows whether this is something mystical—or just a parasite from inland that's reached us. We need to meet Niamh and Milak to finish the smear ritual. Gaea will be safe here at camp. We won't be gone long— maybe an hour."

Mary-Ann stood up and stretched. "Let me check on Gaea. Make sure she's asleep before we go."

****

A sudden growl from my stomach dragged me from a deep sleep.

The noise was so loud, it felt like it could wake the whole forest.

"Okay, okay," I mumbled, pushing myself upright.

The cold air hit my face as I stepped out of the tent, a sharp contrast to the warmth of my sleeping bag. "Mamo? Papo?" I called, but only the rustling leaves answered. Their tent was open, their belongings scattered in a mess that made no sense.

Where did they go? They wouldn't leave me—especially after telling me never to enter the forest alone.

Birds chirped and small animals scurried, but the campfire was just a pile of cold, gray ash. No smell of breakfast, no coffee brewing—just the damp, earthy scent of the forest.

My heart pounded as I walked to the stream. Maybe rinsing my face would help me focus. I bent over, splashing the icy water on my skin, trying to shake off the unease growing in my chest.

They wouldn't leave me. Not like this.

That rumble in my stomach reminded me to eat. I found leftover stew and bread. The meat was cold and tasteless, but the bread helped a little. I looked around, hoping for a note, an explanation of where they'd gone. Nothing. Just a mess.

Maybe if I walk up and down the stream, I might find a clue—it's like a scavenger hunt, only for finding parents, I giggled softly, not yet realizing the truth.

I wandered, searching, calling their names, but only silence answered. "I am free. I am happy. I am loved," I whispered, trying to convince myself.

Hours passed. The sun dipped below the trees, casting long, ominous shadows. I returned to camp, heart pounding.

"Mamo? Papo? Please?"

The air was heavy, charged. A cold shiver ran down my spine, and the feeling of being watched overwhelmed me. I scrambled into their tent, zipped it shut, hands shaking.

"Where are you?" I whispered, tears blurring my vision.

I lay on their mattress, the flickering light casting dancing shadows on the tent walls. Every creak, every rustle made me jump. "Mamo, Papo, please come back." I was so tired, so scared. I closed my eyes for just a moment—and drifted off.

****

A loud crash and heavy thud outside the tent jolted me awake. My heart hammered as I bolted upright.

"Mamo? Papo?" The sun's rays struggled through the giant trees, barely lighting the clearing.

I stumbled out, eyes straining to focus. Then I saw it—a wolf, huge and terrifying, its amber eyes glowing in the dim light.

This is it. My legs froze, my throat tightened. "This is what took them. And it's here for me too," I said aloud.

"No way," a young boy's voice said, clear as day in my head, dripping with disgust. "I don't eat human meat. Gross."

"Who said that?" I whispered, voice trembling.

The wolf shifted, lowering its head like a playful puppy.

"Me," it said. "I can talk to you. Telepathically. It's a shifter thing."

"Shifter?" I repeated, confused and terrified. "Why are you here if not to eat me? And what happened to Mamo and Papo?"

"Ahh, so your parents haven't told you yet," he said sadly. "I'm a shifter — I can shift between human and wolf. We don't eat human meat; it makes us crazy and very ill. As for your parents, Achlys took them."

"Achlys?" I repeated, heart pounding.

"An ancient evil. She took them. You're not safe here. Come with me—hurry."

I was too scared to cry or argue. Clumsily, I packed my things and followed the wolf.

"I'm Cador," he said, bouncing excitedly around me. "I'll be pack leader one day. You're Gaea, right?"

"Yes," I whispered. "How do you know my name?"

"My mom is friends with your father. I'm thirteen. How old are you?" He grinned, still bouncing.

"Ten. Yesterday was my birthday," I said softly.

He led me up a muddy hill to a dark, damp cave. "Stay here," he said. "I'll be back."

"Why can't you just take me home?" I asked, tears stinging my eyes.

"I promise, everything will be explained soon," he said—and then he was gone.

The cave smelled of damp earth and rotting leaves. I rolled out my sleeping bag and curled into a ball, shivering as the darkness pressed in. From the far back of the cave, I heard water dripping into a puddle.

Please come back, I thought. I don't like being alone.

Tired and scared, I drifted off to sleep.

CHAPTER FIVE

"Wake up, sweet child," a soft voice cooed. "Are you hungry?"

A woman stood before me—beautiful and pale, her eyes like the ocean and her hair as white as snow.

"I'm Niamh," she said gently, "Cador's mother."

"But you're not..." I began, confused.

"Yes, child. I am not in my wolf form right now, but I am a shifter like Cador," she explained. "We can be human, wolf, or something in between. The one who took your parents, Achlys... she's a different kind of shifter. Her form shifts between human and panther. Her soul is dark, and she holds no love for anyone—animals or humans alike. She wants to rule everything."

She handed me a handful of berries and some bread. "Here. Eat this. You have a long journey tomorrow. You won't remember anything past falling asleep tonight—until you return to the forest once more. It's a protective gift from Ichicka against Achlys."

Tears welled in my eyes. "Why did Achlys take my parents?"
Niamh's gaze softened. "I cannot tell you now. But one day, when you return as an adult, come find me. I will tell you everything. For now, not knowing keeps you safe."

"Tomorrow morning, one of our pack's most trusted warriors, Milak, will come for you and escort you back to Graceway. You should get some rest."

"Can't I go with you?" I cried.

"It's too dangerous. If Achlys senses you with us, she will come for you. This cave is protected."

****

Dawn painted the cave entrance in soft, gray light.

A large man stood before me, his voice deep and gentle.

"Gaea," he said, "I'm Milak. I'll take you into town."

He was huge, with kind eyes and a stern face. I was too tired and confused to speak, so I just grunted.

We walked in silence for hours. My legs ached, and my stomach grumbled empty. The forest blurred around me—an endless, green maze. Milak was patient, stopping when I stumbled, waiting for me to catch up. He knew I was small, human, and exhausted.

By late afternoon, I could barely walk.

"Stop. I need to rest," I whispered hoarsely. "I'm so hungry and tired."

He nodded. "We can rest. You can sleep while I hunt for food." He gathered wood around us and built a fire.

Hunt? I thought. *Why not just berries and roots?* But I didn't dare question him.

While he was gone, I drifted to sleep, warmth from the fire seeping into my bones.

I woke to the smell of burning flesh—rabbit roasting over the flames. My stomach growled louder.

"Here," Milak said, handing me a piece of meat. "This is the best I could do."

It was bland and chewy, nothing like Mamo's cooking. But I was starving, so I ate, biting off huge chunks like a wild animal.

"How much farther?" I asked, voice weak, with half-chewed food slipping from my mouth.

"About half a day's walk," he replied.

I groaned and fell back asleep. Milak added more wood to the fire and kept watch.

****

"Wake up, girl," Milak said, shaking me gently. "We must go before the sun gets too high."

I woke with a jolt, the crushing pain of losing Mamo and Papo washing over me. The cruel realization that I would never see them again broke me. Tears poured freely.

"I can't. I'm done," I sobbed, collapsing onto the forest floor. "I can't believe they're just gone. I miss them so much."

Milak's voice was soft. "We're almost there, child. We need to get you to Graceway."

But I couldn't stop crying. I curled into a ball, shaking with grief. He let me cry, knowing I needed it.

Eventually, exhaustion claimed me. Milak gently lifted me and carried me the rest of the way.

****

The town was eerily quiet.

It was a Wednesday mid-morning—no one around.

Milak walked to the local park and placed me beneath a giant oak tree.

"You'll be safe here, child," he said, then turned and left.

****

I woke beneath the tree, the town surrounding me.

"What...?" I sat up, disoriented.

Birds chirped, and the diner nearby smelled of greasy food.

Why am I here?

I tried to stand but my legs were weak, my head foggy. Something was wrong.

I walked toward home, confused.

Maybe Papo's meeting with the mayor?

A crowd gathered outside City Hall, news cameras flashing.

Mayor Stein spoke into a microphone.

"We're going to find that little girl," he said.

"I heard she's been gone for almost a week!" a woman shouted.

"They live near the forest," a man said. "Something happened to them."

"Gaea's grandparents are in Sheriff Dontry's office," Mayor Stein added. "We will find out what happened."

They're looking for me?

I pushed through the crowd. "What's going on? Where are my parents?"

People stared, then hugged me, asking questions. I was dazed, confused.

"Please," I said, "tell Papo I'm here."

Sheriff Dontry pushed through the restless crowd and took me to her office.

Grammy cried when she saw me.

"My darling Gaea," she whispered.

"Grammy? Daddo? Why are you here? And where are my parents?" I asked, confused.

"Calm down, Mama," Daddo said. "Let's take her home."

And then the cold, sinking feeling settled deep inside me. Something terrible had happened.

I remembered the camping trip, the stories, the strange dream. And then... nothing.

CHAPTER SIX

Grammy and Daddo were Mamo's parents from Wave Crest. We used to take road trips to visit them, camping at every spot we could find along the way. Those trips were filled with stories, laughter, and stars brighter than anywhere else.

My bathroom only had a shower, so Grammy drew a hot bath for me in my parents' room. She added chamomile and Epsom salts to the water, hoping it would help ease my aching body and restless mind.

The scent of chamomile drifted through the steam like a lullaby— sweet, warm, almost like apples. It wrapped around me, soft and gentle, inviting me in.

When I stepped into the tub, the water burned my feet at first, but then my muscles began to relax, my body slowly surrendering to the warmth. I sank deeper, letting the water rise over my shoulders, my head resting just beneath the surface, ears muffled, heartbeat loud in my chest.

Tears came silently. I didn't fight them. They slid down my cheeks, blending with the bathwater as my thoughts swirled.

I remembered the stream, playing beside it. Dinner with Mamo and Papo. The story Papo told us that night. S'mores by the fire. My first night sleeping in my own tent.

And then... nothing.

The next thing I knew, I was waking up in the middle of town, with no memory of what happened in between.

A knock on the bathroom door pulled me from my thoughts.

"Gaea, dear, are you still okay?" Grammy asked gently.

"I'm fine, thanks, Grammy. Getting out now."

"Okay, sweetheart. I've made dinner. We'll wait for you downstairs."

I sighed, reaching up to comb through my curls. Twigs and dead leaves were tangled in them, stubborn little reminders of the forest. I pulled them out, washed my hair, scrubbed away the dirt, and rinsed off the last traces of the woods.

Grammy had left fresh pajamas folded on the dresser. I slipped into them, the fabric soft against my skin.

The scent of dinner filled the air—baked potatoes, pan-fried pork chops, gravy, and buttery green beans. It smelled like Christmas and comfort and everything good. My stomach growled in response.

After dinner, Grammy tucked me into bed, her hand cool against my forehead. But the peace didn't last. As soon as I closed my eyes, the nightmares returned.

****

The air around my tent turned icy, swirling with invisible wind. A muffled thud. Then silence. Thick. Suffocating.

Something clawed at the tent fabric—scraping, tearing, pressing against it.

Growls.

Shifting shadows.

The foul stench of sulfur burned my nose.

No! Get away from me! I screamed in my mind, frozen, unable to move.

****

I woke up screaming, drenched in sweat, heart pounding like thunder in my chest.

Grammy burst into the room, panic on her face. She rushed to me, wrapping me in her arms.

"My poor child," she whispered, rocking me gently. "Come here. Grammy's got you."

"I don't understand," I sobbed. "What happened to Mamo and Papo? I can't remember. I went to sleep in my tent... and then... I woke up in the park. I'm so scared."

"Shhh, it's okay," she said softly, stroking my hair. "Don't worry about that now. You're safe. We're here."

Daddo came in with a mug of warm milk, his eyes tired and full of love. He handed it to me without a word, just a nod, and sat on the edge of the bed.

They stayed with me until I drifted back to sleep again—Grammy holding my hand, Daddo watching over me like a silent guard.

But even as sleep claimed me, the nightmare lingered... curling like smoke around the edges of my mind.

CHAPTER SEVEN

A year has passed. A year since Mamo and Papo vanished.

Now Grammy and Daddo are taking me away.

I knew this day would come. I didn't blame them. The house had become too quiet—too haunted by memories of laughter and warmth that now lingered like ghosts. To be fair, Grammy and Daddo were never from Graceway. Their home had always called them back to Wave Crest.

At night, I would hear them whispering, their voices low and heavy with worry.

"We need to sell the animals," Daddo said. "And pack up Mary-Ann and Peter's research. It's for Gaea, for when she's older."

"It's time," Grammy agreed, her voice tight. "Even the town's changed. The folks around here look at her like she's a ghost… like she knows something she shouldn't."

A clean start, they said. But all I felt was the sting of another loss.

Not just Mamo and Papo. Not just the unanswered questions. But my animals. My friends. My home.

Wave Crest was a city, a place where none of that could follow me. But I understood. I kept what I could—what truly mattered—and Daddo packed it in boxes for me. The rest, they sold or gave away.

I said my final goodbyes to the farm and climbed into Daddo's old station wagon.

****

The drive felt endless—a heavy, silent journey. Grammy and Daddo took turns driving, their expressions carved from stone. Every familiar landmark we passed stabbed at my heart like a blade.

The field where we played. The trees where we picnicked. The road that led to Ichicka Forest.

Each one was a memory wrapped in pain.

I kept my eyes closed for most of the ride, a tight knot of dread twisting in my stomach. The silence was worse than any argument—thick, suffocating. I only opened my eyes when we stopped for gas or food, and even then, I couldn't look for long. I was afraid I'd see something that would undo me. Something I couldn't bear.

****

Coming to Wave Crest without Mamo and Papo felt... wrong. Before, it had been filled with wonder and excitement. Now it felt cold.

Empty.

Even my memories of Grammy and Daddo's house were bittersweet. I used to camp in their backyard, pretending the fruit trees could talk. I told stories to the squirrels and birds. But now, the animals felt different—distant. As if they didn't recognize me anymore.

The bright lights. The endless crowds. The hurried footsteps and eyes that never lingered.

It was the opposite of Graceway, where everyone knew my name and the wind carried familiar voices. Here, I was a stranger.

The houses stood close together, like boxes stacked in rows. Our sprawling farm was gone. A wave of homesickness crashed over me, sharp and aching.

Daddo was unloading the car when Uncle Donnie from next door walked over.

"Garden's fine, Jer," I heard him say.

"Thanks, mate. I really owe you one," Daddo replied. "BBQ this weekend on me?"

"Sounds good. We'll see you then."

"Later, Donnie."

"Later, Jer."

"Gaea, wake up," Grammy said gently, tapping my shoulder. "We're home."

"Already?" I mumbled, stretching. I wasn't really asleep. Just pretending.

"Come help," she said. I knew they were trying. But all I wanted was to disappear into the silence of my room.

"Can I help with the boxes?" I asked Daddo, stepping out.

"Just your bags," he said softly. "The boxes... they're your parents' things. I'll put them in the attic."

****

I walked past Daddo's prize roses—bright, loud, blooming in every shade. Bees buzzed busily, ignoring the weight in my chest.

Up the front steps and into the familiar house. It was white, with a dark green roof and a porch just big enough for a swing and Daddo's rocking chair.

Inside, it smelled of dust and old wood. It wasn't home.

They'd packed up our lives. Sold the animals. Everything was gone.

I glanced at the wall—and froze. A photo of Mamo, Papo, and me stood in a wooden frame, taken at the border of Ichicka Forest. Mamo was laughing. Papo was pointing to a flower. I looked away, my throat tight. Every picture was a wound that hadn't healed.

The floorboards creaked as I stepped through the living room. Small. Cluttered. The stairs were carpeted in brown—mossy, forest brown.

"Maybe I can decorate my room. New colors. New bedding for a new me," I thought, climbing slowly. *"Make it feel... less like this."*

My room was tiny—half the size of my old one. No bathroom. Just a single window that overlooked a small garden patch, swallowed by a sea of concrete. A bed. A desk. A closet.

My suitcase thudded onto the floor, heavy with pieces of a past life.

"I'll unpack later," I muttered and headed back downstairs.

****

"Sorry, Daddo," I said as I passed him on the stairs. He was carrying a box labeled *Mary-Ann & Peter's Research #1*.

"It's okay," he replied, voice tired. "Just putting these in the attic. For when you're older."

The attic stairs were tucked behind a door, narrow and creaky. The air smelled like dust and memories.

Sunlight streamed through the small round window, casting long beams where dust danced like tiny ghosts.

I'll just put them here, Daddo thought, placing the box in the far corner. *Maybe she'll want them someday.*

CHAPTER EIGHT

"How about tacos for dinner, ladies?" Daddo asked, a hopeful lilt in his voice.

"Pepe's, by the beach?" Grammy replied, her eyes lighting up.

"Yes!" I shouted, throwing my arms around him. "Thank you, Daddo!" It had been so long since I felt excited about anything.

The drive to Pepe's was a blur of lights, like scattered stars on a velvet sky. "It's so beautiful," I breathed, rolling the window down to let the salty ocean air wash over me. "Can we walk on the beach after?"

"Not tonight, love," Daddo said. "But soon, I promise."

Pepe's was a splash of color against the night—bright tables, flickering lanterns, the air thick with the scent of spices and sea breeze. A skinny teenager named Chris took our order.

"Pulled pork tacos," I said, my mouth already watering. "And a cherry cola!"

"Same," Grammy chimed in.

Daddo ordered the same too, but with regular cola. He gave me a warm, quiet smile—happy to see me happy, even if only for a moment.

We chatted about random things, anything to keep the shadows of memory from creeping in. For the first time in a long while, I laughed out loud.

The tacos arrived, piled high with smoky pork and bright salsa. I savored every bite, juice dripping down my chin.

"These are amazing," I mumbled between mouthfuls.

Then, with sudden courage, I spoke: "Daddo, Grammy… can we decorate my room? I want to take this new life as an adventure, and I want to start with my space."

"Of course, my angel," Daddo said, his voice tender.

Chris cleared our plates and brought the check. The car ride home was quiet and warm, the scent of tacos lingering in the air. I fell asleep with my head against the window, exhausted but content.

****

"She's been through so much," Grammy—Mandy—whispered later that night.

"Lizzy had some pets up for adoption," Daddo—Jerry—said thoughtfully. "Maybe we could take Gaea to visit. Let her choose one."

41

"That's a wonderful idea," Grammy replied. "It might help. Might even bring her a little peace."

"I think we should help her settle into her room first. I'll get the paint out, and you can take her shopping for new bedding."

"Yes, that's a great idea." Mandy smiled. "You really are such a wonderful granddad."

They drove home in silence, hearts a little lighter.

****

The next morning, Daddo took me to his garage workshop.

"Paint colors," he said, laying out swatches like treasure maps.

"Choose anything your heart desires. And if it's not here, we'll mix until we find the perfect one."

I chose **crystal white** for the walls and **lilac** for the trims and corners. And most important—**glow-in-the-dark stars** for the ceiling.

Later, Grammy and I went shopping for new bedding and curtains while Daddo and some young guys from the neighborhood painted my room. It was strange but fun—Graceway didn't have malls, and everything felt new and exciting.

Grammy took me to her favorite coffee shop. I had a chocolate milkshake and a slice of black forest cake. She had a steaming cup of coffee and a slice of carrot cake.

Afterward, we stopped by a clothing store where Grammy got me new pajamas, fluffy slippers, and a few extra things "just because."

At the end of the mall was a massive bedding store called *Snooze*. It had everything—curtains, duvets, pillows, and cozy throws.

I chose a deep purple duvet with lilac lace trim. It reminded me of the early morning sky, just before the sun spills its first light across the world.

We even picked out a **bigger bed**. "They'll deliver this one," Grammy said with a wink, "and we'll donate the old one."

****

When we got home, my room was nearly done.

"That was fast," I said, surprised.

"Plenty of helping hands," Daddo replied with a proud smile. "I kept some of your old furniture and just gave it a good polish and fresh paint. A mix of old and new. Just like life."

I stood in the doorway of my room—*my* room—feeling something I hadn't in a long time.

Hope.

CHAPTER NINE

""Up, sleepyhead," Daddo said gently from my doorway. "Breakfast. We have a surprise."

I groaned, pulling the covers over my head. "School starts on Monday. Can't I sleep in while I still can?"

"This is better than sleep," he promised, and disappeared downstairs.

I dragged myself out of bed, dressed quickly, and shuffled down to the kitchen. Toast and milk. Not Grammy's usual breakfast feast. "Surprise?" I asked, rubbing my eyes. "Please tell me we're not moving again."

"No, no," Daddo chuckled. "We're going to Lizzy's. You like her animals, don't you?"

Lizzy's Safe Haven—the animal shelter. A flicker of excitement sparked inside me. I missed animals. Their warm fur. Their soft sounds. Their unconditional love.

"Yes!" I said, suddenly wide awake. "Let's go!"

"Eat first, then we'll go," Grammy said, placing a plate in front of me.

Her fresh-baked sourdough, my favorite—just like Mamo used to make. I spread butter thickly and added a dollop of her homemade strawberry jam. It tasted like sunshine and memory. I washed it down with a cold glass of milk and licked the jam from my lips.

****

Lizzy met us at the door, her smile warm and bright.

"Hi, Gaea," she said. "It's been a while."

"Hi, Aunt Lizzy."

"Please," she laughed, "just Lizzy. 'Aunt' makes me feel ancient. Come on—they're waiting."

The shelter smelled like something clean and sharp, like disinfectant mixed with fur. We passed a girl with bright blue hair who gave me a cheerful wave.

"This is Siggy, my new receptionist," Lizzy said.

"Hi," Siggy said. Her voice matched her hair—bright and energetic.

Double steel doors opened into a world of barking, tail wags, and curious eyes. Dogs of every size and shape looked out at us from their kennels, some excited, some shy, all hopeful.

"Where are the people?" I asked, scanning the empty corridor.

"Just us," Lizzy said with a grin. "And them." She gestured to the animals. "You're choosing a companion."

"Really?" My heart leaped. "Can I choose anyone?"

"With rules," Daddo said, his voice firm but kind. "Feeding, cleaning, playing—everything. Your responsibility."

"Yes, yes!" I said, practically bouncing. "I promise!"

"We'll start in the back," Lizzy said, leading us through a quieter hallway.

We entered the cattery. The soft scent of litter and fur filled the air. Purring cats lounged in hammocks, stretched on cushions, or padded softly between our legs. Ginger cats, gray ones, even a few with bright eyes and crooked tails.

But one caught my attention—a massive, smoky gray Maine Coon with golden eyes and a lion's ruff of fur.

"Mr. Purwinkle," Lizzy said. "He's a gentle giant. Been here for almost a year. A little older, but endlessly sweet."

I knelt beside him, running my hands through his thick coat. He flopped onto his side, then his back, belly up and purring so loudly it rumbled through my fingertips.

"He's perfect," I whispered. "Can we take him home, Daddo?"

"If you promise to take care of him," Daddo said, his eyes searching mine.

"I will," I said, heart swelling with certainty. "I really will."

While Daddo and Lizzy went to fill out the paperwork, I stayed with Mr. Purwinkle. He lay sprawled across my legs, his paws kneading the air as I stroked his back.

"I'll take care of you forever," I whispered, pressing my cheek to his warm fur.

He purred louder, and something deep inside me stirred—**a sense of purpose**. A feeling I hadn't felt in a long, long time.

CHAPTER TEN

It was my first day at a new school, and I was glad Grammy and Daddo had waited until the new school year to enroll me. At least now I wouldn't be the *only* new kid.

Wave Crest Private School was a K–12 school—meaning everything from kindergarten to high school was packed onto the same sprawling property. It felt strange. I'd always been homeschooled, so being surrounded by so many kids was overwhelming.

They gathered in clusters, like little ecosystems of their own. The popular ones. The sporty ones. The loud ones. And the quiet ones— people like me. Loners.

Everyone was friendly enough, smiling in the hallways or offering help when I looked lost. But I kept mostly to myself. I knew why I was here. I had a dream. I wanted to become a wildlife veterinarian, like Papo. I wanted to save animals. And maybe… maybe one day return home.

The hallways buzzed with life—lockers slamming, sneakers squeaking, voices overlapping like a sea of sound. Everyone looked the same… but also different. Confident. Loud. Settled.

The day went by in a blur of new names and unfamiliar classrooms. When the final bell rang at 3:00 PM, I rushed outside, and there he was—Daddo, leaning against the car, sunglasses on and smiling.

"Hi, Daddo!" I said, climbing into the passenger seat with a tired grin.

"Hi, Gaea. So—how was your first day on this new adventure?"

"It was… okay, I guess," I said, shrugging off my backpack. "The kids are friendly, and the teachers seem nice. It's just… a lot."

"I know it's hard," he said, pulling out of the parking lot, "but I promise—it gets better. In the end, you'll make a success of it. I know this much is true."

"Thanks, Daddo. I'll definitely give it my best." I paused. "Where's Grammy?"

"You know the old girl—always has something to bake or cook for someone," he chuckled, shaking his head. "She says it keeps her young."

When we got home, there was no homework—one of the rare gifts of a first day. I changed into comfy clothes and spent the afternoon playing with Mr. Purwinkle. He purred like a tractor and followed me around the house, pawing at my legs and rubbing his face against my socks.

Later, we all had dinner together—lasagna, garlic bread, and Grammy's cucumber salad. We laughed, talked about my classes, and shared stories until my eyes started drooping.

When I finally crawled into bed, Mr. Purwinkle curled up beside me, warm and heavy.

That night, I slept like a stone.

A perfect, dreamless night.

CHAPTER ELEVEN

Beep beep.

The alarm clock's shrill cry was the unwelcome soundtrack to my mornings.

"Seven years," I muttered, slamming the snooze button. "Seven years of private school, and I still can't get used to this infernal noise."

I missed Mamo's soft wake-up calls—the warm scent of hot cocoa drifting up the stairs, her gentle voice laced with love. Those were the mornings that felt like magic.

I stumbled into the bathroom. My uniform hung neatly on the back of the door, like a waiting ghost. Routine: tie back my hair, wash my face, brush my teeth. Even the toothpaste was too minty this morning— sharp, like everything else lately.

Saturday is my birthday. Eighteen.

A milestone, they say. But all I could think about was *what comes next*—the will, the farm. It would all be mine now. Even though I didn't want it, I couldn't sell it either. Family tradition. Legacy. Burden. The attorney would be arriving soon, with papers to sign. The future, sealed in ink.

I trudged downstairs.

"Whoa there, slow down," Daddo said with a chuckle as I nearly missed the last step.

"Morning, Daddo," I mumbled, rubbing my eyes. "I'm going to miss the bus."

"Wait a second," he said, raising a hand with a knowing grin. "We've got something for you."

I frowned, confused, but followed him out the front door. Grammy stood waiting on the porch, her smile brighter than the morning sun.

Daddo handed me a key.

"What's this?" I asked, examining it. It looked like a car key... but not to his ancient station wagon.

"It's exactly what you think it is," Daddo said, his eyes twinkling.

And then I saw it.

A small, red two-door car parked at the end of the driveway— gleaming in the light, like something out of a dream.

"But... how? Is it really mine?" The words tumbled out, caught between disbelief and joy.

"It's yours," Grammy said, her voice warm and proud. "It's not brand new, but it runs perfectly. We sold the last of the farm furniture and the animals. You've worked hard—at school, at Lizzy's. You earned this."

"And since you passed your driver's ed last month," Daddo added, "we figured it was the right time."

Tears stung my eyes. "So much has happened," I whispered. "But I'm so thankful for you both."

I walked to the car, my fingers trailing over its cool, smooth surface. A piece of freedom. A symbol of everything changing.

"Bye, guys! See you after my shift at Lizzy's! I love you!" I called, sliding behind the wheel.

The interior smelled faintly of pine. A tree-shaped air freshener hung from the mirror, reminding me of Ichika Forest—a place that now felt like a memory wrapped in mist.

I took a breath, started the engine, and eased out of the driveway. Uncle Donnie waved from his porch as I passed, and I waved back, a small smile tugging at my lips.

The car purred. It wasn't fast or flashy, but it was *mine*.

By the time I reached school, I was a few minutes late. I parked, slipped through the massive glass doors, and let the weight of routine settle over me.

The hallways stretched in pale vinyl and fluorescent glare. Reception. Headmaster's office. Lockers and kids. It was a school like any other—and yet, still so far from home.

The bell rang. I ducked into my first class, my mind already drifting. At lunch, I escaped to my usual spot under the old oak tree. The rustle of leaves above was more comforting than any voice in the cafeteria. Friendly as they were, the other students felt like shadows passing through a life I didn't fully belong to.

"Studying," I'd say when they asked. The truth was simpler: I needed the quiet. I had a goal—wildlife veterinarian. And I wasn't going to let distractions derail that dream.

After school, I headed to Lizzy's.

"Nice ride," Siggy called as I pulled in. Her electric-blue hair popped against the clinic's white walls like a splash of rebellion.

"Thanks, Sigs," I said, locking the car. "Quiet day?"

"Quiet *enough*," she said with a shrug. "Lizzy's out on a call—something at the Wave Crest sanctuary."

"Have you ever been there?"

"Just the tourist park side. The research center's way more secretive. They hardly let anyone in. Super weird, if you ask me."

"Very," I agreed.

The rest of the afternoon passed in a familiar rhythm—puppy cuddles, cleaning, flipping through textbooks. Comforting. Ordinary. But as the sky turned gold and I stepped out the front door, a sudden chill ran down my spine.

I froze.

A tingling sensation crawled over my skin, like static—or like a cold breath at the back of my neck.

I turned slowly.

And saw him.

Across the road, standing beside a gray truck, was a tall figure. Easily over six feet. Long, dark hair falling past his shoulders. He wasn't moving—just *watching*.

His face was shadowed, but his eyes—amber, glowing faintly like embers in the dusk—held mine. Unblinking. Intense. Almost... inhuman.

A pulse of recognition stirred somewhere deep inside me. But I couldn't place it.

Then he turned. Slowly. Deliberately. Climbed into the truck. Even as he pulled away, his eyes never left mine.

I stood rooted to the spot, heart hammering.

Who was he? Why did he feel familiar? And why did he look at me like he already knew me?

I shook my head, trying to chase the lingering unease. Probably just a big-city weirdo passing through. Nothing to panic about.

Still, as I climbed into my car and drove home, the image of those eyes followed me like a shadow.

I didn't tell Grammy or Daddo. I didn't want to worry them. But I couldn't shake the feeling that something had just... shifted.

CHAPTER TWELVE

Saturday finally arrived—my birthday. The day I had been dreading for years.

The scent of vanilla and cinnamon drifted from the kitchen, warm and comforting, tugging gently at the edges of my sadness. Grammy was baking—birthday cake, no doubt. Through the kitchen window, I saw Daddo moving things around in the backyard.

They're planning something, I thought, exhaling a quiet sigh. *I told them I just wanted a quiet day.*

I stepped into the shower, letting the hot water wash over me, rinsing away the weight of old grief and the strange unease that clung to my skin like a second layer. When I stepped out, I dressed slowly—new jeans and a black T-shirt decorated with tiny, sparkling flowers. A small act of rebellion against the heaviness inside me.

As I passed the mirror, I paused.

I rarely looked at myself—*really* looked. But this morning, I couldn't help it. The young woman staring back felt like a stranger.

My jeans hugged my waist. My shirt outlined curves I hadn't paid attention to before. My eyes, once full of soft innocence, now held something sharper. Loss, maybe. Or something deeper.

I didn't know who I was becoming. But I knew I wasn't the same girl anymore.

"Morning, Grammy," I said, stepping into the kitchen.

Grammy nearly dropped her mixing bowl.

"You look beautiful," she said softly, her voice edged with emotion. "If only your parents could see you now."

I looked away. "No guests, okay? Please."

"Eighteen is a milestone, young lady," she replied firmly. "We're celebrating. Whether you like it or not."

The doorbell rang before I could argue.

"Get that, will you?" she said, waving her spoon.

I opened the door.

A short, bald man stood on the porch. He wore a crisp grey suit, and his neatly trimmed mustache framed a mouth set in a professional line. But his eyes—dark and sharp—held an unreadable intensity.

"Gaea Angevin?" he asked.

"Yes," I said cautiously.

"Mr. Schultz. Attorney for your parents' estate." He handed me a thick stack of documents. "I'll need your signature for the release of your inheritance."

"Oh. Um... okay. Please, come in," I said, leading him to the living room. "I'll get Grammy and Daddo—"

"This is for you only," he interrupted, his tone firm but not unkind. "The farm must remain in the Angevin bloodline and cannot be sold. It is legally bound to your family and directly tied to the forest—Ichicka—which you are also inheriting. All of it now passes to you."

I blinked. "The *forest*? Wait—Ichicka? The whole thing? But... why?"

"It's all explained in a letter your father left behind," he said, pulling a thick, sealed envelope from his briefcase. "For your eyes only. Sealed by law. The estate funds and land titles will be officially transferred to your name once the documents are signed."

He stood abruptly.

"We'll send you copies of everything. Enjoy your day, Miss Angevin."

"Wait—questions," I said, stumbling after him as he walked toward the door.

"Read the letter," he replied without turning. And with that, he stepped outside and disappeared down the path.

I closed the door slowly, dazed.

Across the street, I spotted it again. The grey truck.

Parked in the same spot as before, its tinted windows catching the sunlight like twin black mirrors.

I stepped out onto the porch. But it was already pulling away.

"Imagining things," I whispered, even though my pulse had quickened. I forced myself back inside.

The envelope felt heavier than it should have. Like it carried not just words, but the weight of a legacy—one I never asked for.

I climbed the stairs to the attic. Dust swirled in the air, catching in my throat. The scent of old wood and forgotten memories clung to the beams like ghosts.

I didn't turn on the light.

I placed the letter and legal documents on an old box and stood there for a moment, frozen.

Then I turned and left without opening it.

Not yet.

CHAPTER THIRTEEN

The doorbell rang.

"Get that, please, love," Grammy called from the kitchen, still busy preparing snacks.

It was Lizzy and Siggy—the first to arrive.

I adored Siggy. She had an otherworldly charm that always made her feel like she belonged to another dimension entirely. Her hair, a kaleidoscope of ever-changing hues, was always styled with striking, modern flair. Today, it was a vibrant neon pink, cropped into a bold pixie cut. The sharpness of her hair contrasted with her outfit—a flowing black skirt, a simple tank top, and a floor-length, lacy black jacket that fluttered like shadowed silk. Her eyeliner, also pink, was drawn into dramatic, feline points that emphasized her long, faux lashes.

Lizzy, as always, grounded the moment—plain denim jeans, a clean white T-shirt, and a smile that felt like home.

"Hi, ladies. Glad you could make it," I said, hugging them both.

"Glad to be here," Siggy smiled.

"Ditto," Lizzy grinned.

Uncle Donnie arrived just as they stepped inside. His quiet presence was comforting. Widowed after his wife's tragic childbirth, he had raised his son alone. But now his boy lived far away, and their visits were rare.

"Hi, Uncle Donnie. Welcome," I said, stepping aside. "Daddo's in the backyard."

I led them all through the house to where the celebration was unfolding.

These were the moments I treasured. Simple. Honest. A small, close-knit gathering of people who loved each other.

I sat for a moment and took it all in, soaking up the scene like sunlight: Daddo, brow furrowed in concentration, tending to the barbecue as the smoky aroma of grilling meat drifted through the air. Uncle Donnie beside him, their low voices a gentle hum beneath the breeze. Grammy carefully arranging snacks on the outdoor table, her movements slow but practiced. Lizzy and Siggy's laughter echoing in the open space, warm and unrestrained. Even old Mr. Purwinkle had made it—frail, sleepy, but present. A small miracle.

Only Mamo and Papo were missing. A familiar ache tightened in my chest.

"No," I whispered to myself, brushing the thought away. "Not today. Today, I choose joy."

I stood up and joined my friends, letting their laughter lift me. It wrapped around me like a blanket, softening the sharp edges of memory.

Grammy came outside, holding a large vanilla cake. The frosting was a swirl of soft purple, lilac petals blooming across its surface. The candles flickered in the breeze, their flames dancing in her eyes as she began to sing.

"Happy birthday to you…"

Everyone joined in—off-key and beaming. Their voices were a messy, beautiful chorus of affection.

I felt my cheeks flush. I had never cared for the spotlight. But this? This was different. These were my people. This was my moment. And for the first time in a long time, I felt whole.

CHAPTER FOURTEEN

My eyes burned, the words on the page blurring into an unintelligible mess. *Time for a break,* I thought, rubbing my temples.

The soft glow of my desk lamp cast long shadows over the stacks of textbooks and notes—a testament to the hours I'd spent hunched in concentration. Glancing at my watch, I winced.

Past 10:00 p.m.

Grammy and Daddo were probably asleep, but my throat was parched and my stomach growled in protest. I slipped downstairs, the wooden steps creaking softly beneath my feet. In the kitchen, I rummaged through the fridge and pulled out some leftovers, grabbing a bottle of water before heading back upstairs.

Exams loomed—a three-week marathon of written and practical tests. Six years. Six years of grueling commutes between their house, the university, and Lizzy's apartment. It hadn't been easy. But the thought of finally having my own place—a quiet sanctuary between school and work—kept me going.

I didn't *need* the money anymore. My inheritance had changed that. But knowing that I'd saved enough to buy it myself, piece by piece, with the small jobs I took on during breaks... That meant something. That was mine.

I earned this.

Two years of a certified herbalist course, now nearing the end of a four-year veterinary degree. *Next year—the master's,* I thought, a surge of excitement flickering through the fog of fatigue. Wildlife veterinary medicine.

The idea of working with exotic animals, tending to them in the wild, traveling between nature reserves, zoos, and conservation camps— with Lizzy by my side—gave me a profound sense of purpose. Not just *healing*, but *protecting.*

I was eyeing a two-bedroom duplex with a small yard near Siggy's place. Perfect location. I could picture it already: the scent of wildflowers drifting through open windows, a gentle breeze rustling the trees. A hammock in the yard. Maybe a little herb garden. Peaceful. Personal. Free.

Mr. Purwinkle would've loved it—especially the hammock. A soft smile curved my lips at the thought, a quiet ache nestled beneath the fondness.

I should talk to Lizzy, I thought. *Maybe I could take a short break before finals to start packing.* The idea of finally having my own space, my own rhythm, my own walls humming with silence and sunlight...

It made the late nights, the cramped buses, and the endless lectures seem—almost—worth   it.

CHAPTER FIVETEEN

The weekend before exams, I decided to tackle the attic. *Time to face the past,* I thought, pulling on a pair of jeans, an old T-shirt, and my scuffed sneakers.

Grammy and Daddo were in the kitchen, the familiar scent of coffee and toast curling through the air like a warm embrace.

"Morning," I said, heading to the fridge. "I'm going to sort through Mom and Dad's things. Start packing for the move."

"You don't have to rush," Daddo said gently.

"We love having you here," Grammy added, her eyes soft but a little sad.

I kissed them both, a familiar ache blooming in my chest. "I know," I said. "But I'm twenty-six. It's time to find my own place. And the master's... there's travel involved."

I grabbed a water bottle and an apple. "Attic time," I called as I made my way upstairs.

The stairs creaked under my feet, every step echoing with memories. Daddo had replaced the old string switch with a proper light years ago, casting a sterile glow over the attic. It wasn't as dusty as I remembered. A faint scent of old paper mingled with the dry, earthy undertone that always lingered up here.

The boxes were stacked neatly in the far corner, each one lightly coated in a fine greyish dust, undisturbed for years. Sitting atop the stack was the enormous yellow envelope, boldly marked:

"Attention: Gaea Angevin."

I brushed the dust off with a swipe of my hand, fingers lingering on the thick paper. *Not yet,* I thought. *First, the boxes.*

I pulled them into a loose circle around me—Mamo's research on my left, Papo's on the right—and sat cross-legged in the center like I was about to perform a ritual.

I opened the first box:

"Mary-Ann's Research 1."

Inside were hundreds of pages—beautifully handwritten remedies, delicate plant illustrations, and notes that made my herbalist instincts buzz with curiosity. Some of the plants I recognized from the forest, others I had never seen before. The drawings were stunning, each leaf and petal shaded with care, veins mapped like tiny highways of life.

This could be useful, I thought, flipping through pages that felt almost sacred.

Then I opened the second box:

"Mary-Ann's Research 2."

The air shifted. A sharp, sulfurous odor hit me like a warning. Inside were sealed petri dishes labeled in bold red: **"TOXIC."**
I wrinkled my nose. I had never seen anything like these on the farm.

Stacked beside them were twelve old diaries, their covers cracked and edges worn. I opened the first one, and soon found myself lost in the pages—notes, sketches, cryptic symbols. Mamo's words were strange at times, intense, even feverish. There were mentions of *Ichicka,* of energies and reactions, warnings about mixing certain roots with river herbs under a full moon. It wasn't just science. There was something else here—something older.
Hours passed.

I looked up and stretched, legs stiff from sitting cross-legged for so long. Five more boxes sat quietly, labeled:

"Peter's Research."

But I'd had enough for one day.

From downstairs, the smoky scent of Daddo's barbecue wafted up through the vents, a tempting distraction.

Still, my eyes drifted back to the yellow envelope. It felt heavier than paper should—weighted not by ink, but by expectation.

I carried it downstairs and placed it on my desk, the surface now cluttered with notes and books. *Later,* I told myself.

Food first. And maybe—after dinner, after peace—I'd finally read the letter that might change everything.

As I stood, my legs prickled with pins and needles, a physical echo of the tension brewing in my chest.

CHAPTER SIXTEEN

Moving day finally arrived.

Boxes were piled high as the **Speedy Movers** truck waited for the last load. The morning buzzed with motion—doors swinging open, tape being torn, footsteps up and down the porch steps. Just as I shoved one last box onto the stack, Mr. Jones, the mailman, approached with a long envelope in hand.

"Good morning, Miss Angevin. Special delivery from WC University."

My heart leapt. I nearly dropped the box. "Thank you, Mr. Jones!"

I tore the envelope open right there on the sidewalk. "I got in!" I shouted, laughing. "I got in!"

Grammy emerged from the front door holding two handcrafted lamps. "In what, my dear?" she asked, squinting as she walked over.

"The master's program!" I beamed. "Wildlife veterinary training!"

Her eyes welled up with tears. She handed the lamps to one of the movers and wrapped her arms around me.

"I'm proud of you, my dear. You've worked so hard for this," she said, voice thick with emotion.

"Jerry!" she called back into the house. "Come say goodbye! The movers just left!"

"I'll visit," I promised as Daddo stepped outside. My throat tightened. "Weekly dinners—unless I'm on call. Love you both."

"We love you too," Daddo said, his voice hoarse.

I loaded the last bag into my car, gave them each one more hug, and climbed into the driver's seat. As I pulled away, exhilaration surged through me. New beginnings. My duplex waited—*my* place. A fresh start.

By the time I arrived, the movers were already unloading. Siggy stood on the porch, waving excitedly with Mike at her side.

"Hi, neighbor!" Siggy grinned, pulling me into a hug. "Remember Mike?"

"Of course!" I said, shaking his hand. "Your wedding, two years ago."

Mike, always reserved, handed me a small keyring. "We got you a wolf keychain," he said with a dry chuckle. "For your studies."

I laughed, touched. "It's perfect."

"Need help unpacking?" Siggy offered.

"Nah, I'm good. Just going to make the bed, order food, and crash."

"Alright, but call if you need anything," she said as they headed out.

I stood surrounded by boxes—*my* boxes. *My* mess. The duplex was a soft baby blue with a navy-blue roof, the afternoon light casting long, golden shadows through the windows. It felt open. Light. Mine.

I ordered tacos and a cherry cola from Pepe's and stepped out into the small garden to wait. The breeze rustled the hedges. I sat in the grass, inhaling the scent of jasmine and soil.

Then it hit me—that prickling unease. Someone was watching.

I looked up.

Across the street stood a tall figure. My stomach dropped. *Him.*

The man from Lizzy's. He was already crossing the street.

A flicker of alarm ran through me... but it wasn't just fear. There was something else. Something deeper. Drawn.

He was striking—tall and broad-shouldered, his tanned skin glowing in the afternoon light. Long, dark hair framed a face carved with intensity. His eyes... were they glowing? Amber. Fierce. Hypnotic.

Snap out of it, I told myself.

He smelled faintly of cedarwood and vetiver, earthy and familiar in a way that unsettled me.

****

It's her.

She looked the same, but more radiant. More alive. I hadn't seen her in months, but I'd never stopped watching. Niamh had warned me—*stay away from this human.*

Why her?

The others—Graceway's women—they were dull. Predictable. Like overripe fruit left too long on the vine. Easy to pluck, but tasteless. I came to Wave Crest to study agriculture, to prepare for leadership—but then I saw *her.*

The first time was outside Lizzy's café. Her presence struck me like lightning to the soul, something ancient stirring within me. Something lost and now… found.

Since then, I'd been a shadow. Always watching, always drawn. She saw me, once. After that, I stayed farther away.

When I told Niamh about her, she'd turned cold. Her voice was sharp—*Off-limits.* No reason. Just a decree. I was meant to lead the pack. Meant to have a mate strong enough to anchor me.

But Niamh… she took her secrets to the grave when Achlys claimed her.

Still, I never forgot the girl. And now… here she was.

****

"Hi," he said, his voice deep and rough. "Sorry for staring. I've seen you around Wave Crest's campus, and I've been wanting to say hello but… I'm a bit awkward with this kind of thing. I'm Cador."

"Hi," I replied, an uneasy laugh escaping me. "Gaea. I thought I recognized you. I was starting to think you were a stalker or something."

"Yeah," he admitted, rubbing the back of his neck. "I get that. Sorry."

Just then, a delivery bike pulled up. *Saved by tacos,* I thought in relief.

"Well," I said, turning to the driver. "Nice meeting you, Cador, but I'm starving and wiped out."

"Of course. No problem. Have a good evening, Gaea. I hope to see you again soon."

I took the bag from the driver, but as I turned, I lost my footing and nearly fell.

From the corner of my eye, I caught a brief, amused smile playing on Cador's lips as he turned and walked back to his truck..

CHAPTER SEVENTEEN

The wildlife veterinary master's program was a blend of lectures and fieldwork. Today's assignment brought us to the WC Wildlife Sanctuary—one of my favorite places—made even better because Lizzy was my mentor. I could be myself around her. She was a powerhouse, juggling a clinic, a shelter, and her own master's degree—all before turning thirty-five.

Our patient: a malnourished, injured wolf found limping near Wave Crest. A strange sight—wolves usually stayed deep within Ichika Forest, further south. But lately, lone wolves had been turning up, sick or hurt, always alone. Lizzy had mentioned wanting to study the pattern, but she was swamped with responsibilities.

"I remember my dad's research on wolf populations," I said, the pickup bouncing along a dusty backroad. "Maybe there's something in his notes. I'll dig through them later, see if I can find anything useful."

I reviewed the wolf's report while we drove—the road a bumpy rollercoaster—and tried to steady both the papers and my thoughts.

As we pulled up to the sanctuary, a tall, familiar figure stepped into view.

"Hi, Cador," Lizzy called, hopping down from the truck. "This is Gaea."

"Hi, Liz. Good to see you again." His amber gaze landed on mine. "Gaea and I have met… in passing."

In passing? More like *on my front lawn*, I thought, pushing the memory aside. *Focus, Gaea. You're here for the wolf, not to indulge your ego.*

"Hi," I said, voice tighter than intended.

We walked through the main doors, the cool rush of air-conditioning a welcome relief from the Wave Crest heat. The building was newer and more spacious than Lizzy's rescue center—wide hallways, high ceilings, gleaming floors. It felt more like a research lab than a shelter.

"Cador," I said, curiosity getting the better of me, "why are you here? I thought you studied agriculture."

"Gaea!" Lizzy gently scolded. "We're here to help, not interrogate."

Cador chuckled, easy and unbothered. "No offense taken. It's a fair question. My team's studying potential diseases wolves might carry— things that could affect livestock. The farmers back in Graceway are worried. It could mean major loss for the entire region."

"Oh." I felt slightly foolish. "That makes sense."

"I like your skepticism," he said, a flicker of amusement in his eyes. "This way—the wolf's sedated."

The wolf's room was large and clean, almost clinical. Glass walls enclosed a space that looked like an oversized kennel. Inside, the creature lay curled on soft straw bedding, ribs sharply outlined beneath fur the color of dried leaves. His paws were massive.

"He's beautiful," I whispered.

"I'll take blood," I said, tying a tourniquet around his leg with practiced ease. The fur was softer than expected. His breathing was shallow, but steady.

"Poor thing," I murmured. "Why would you stray so far?"

Cador stood nearby, quiet, his scent—cedarwood and something untamed—mixing with the sterile air.

"Has he eaten or had any water since being brought in?" I asked, glancing over my shoulder.

"Not really. Just a drip. He was a bit aggressive at first, so we had to sedate him. Might've been dehydration—or hunger. Hopefully he'll wake up soon and be in better shape."

I nodded, filling the vial with blood. "I'll run a panel and compare the results with notes from my dad's old journals. There might be a connection."

"I remember your father," Cador said quietly.

I paused, brow furrowed. "You knew him?"

He hesitated, then nodded. "I'm from Graceway. He used to treat our animals. He was friends with my mother." A pause. "I didn't mean to upset you."

Then he turned sharply and walked out—no goodbye.

I blinked, surprised.

"Well, *someone* has a crush," Lizzy teased, nudging me.

"Don't be ridiculous," I muttered, feeling heat rush to my face. "I'm focused on the job."

Still... his eyes. That voice. I shook the thoughts away. I am not getting attached.

I looked down at the wolf, resting quietly beneath my fingers. "You'll be okay," I whispered, stroking his fur. "I'll find out what happened to you."

CHAPTER EIGHTEEN

We got back to the shelter around 5:00 p.m.

"I'll start with the bloodwork and lock up when I'm done," I said, slipping into work mode.

"Okay, thanks," Lizzy replied. "See you at Siggy's?"

"Not tonight. I'm digging through Dad's journals—maybe he noted something about the wolves of Ichika Forest."

"Don't stay too late," she warned, grabbing her bag. "Get some sleep."

"I'll try. Say hi to Siggy."

Once she left, I settled in at the microscope, placing the wolf's blood sample on the slide. Something felt off almost immediately. The red blood cells... they weren't behaving normally. They looked like they were attacking each other.

That wasn't right.

I added a drop of variation night solution—a standard test for viral markers. No reaction.

Not a virus.

And it wasn't something he ate either—whatever this was, it wasn't digestive in origin. Something deeper. Cellular. Maybe genetic?

My pulse quickened. This was bigger than a malnourished wolf. Dad's journals. I needed to dig deeper.

I sealed and stored the rest of the samples, switched off the lab lights, and stepped outside. The sun had just dipped beneath the ocean line. A warm coastal breeze carried the scent of salt and the distant crash of waves.

Then… that scent again.

Cedarwood.

My skin prickled. My cheeks flushed.

"Hi again," said a deep voice behind me.

I turned sharply, startled. "Are you following me? Because it's creepy, just so you know."

Cador smiled, hands raised in mock surrender. "Sorry. I just—can I take you to dinner? I'd like to get to know you."

"I have plans. Dinner with Lizzy," I lied quickly.

He laughed. "Siggy's? Lizzy told me you weren't coming, so I canceled too. I think she's trying to play matchmaker."

I groaned. "I'm going to kill her."

"Beach walk, then? Milkshakes? No strings attached," he offered with a half-smile that made my heart flutter against my will.

I hesitated, then nodded. "Fine. No strings."

I drove myself and agreed to meet him there. *Lizzy, you're so dead.*

Even if he *was* gorgeous.

Still… I reminded myself firmly, *I'm not looking. I'm not getting attached.*

And someone like him? Definitely out of my league.

CHAPTER NINETEEN

The waves crashed against the shore, a soothing rhythm carried by the cool night breeze. Salt and seaweed hung in the air. I hadn't been to the beach in such a long time. After my parents disappeared, I avoided things that reminded me of them—especially places like this.

"It's a lovely evening," I said, my voice just above a whisper. "Thank you for suggesting this. Even though I was reluctant... my mind needed the distraction." The sand was soft and cool beneath my feet, grounding me in the present.

"I love it here," I continued. "I never thought Wave Crest would grow on me so much. But I still miss Graceway a little—the quiet life, the nature."

"Where in Graceway did you say you lived?" I asked, turning toward him.

"I lived with my mom on one of the smaller farms, on the edge of the city, near Ichicka. Close to the school," he replied.

I nodded slowly, but a flicker of doubt passed through me. Something about his answer felt... not quite right. I didn't remember him, though he felt oddly familiar. "I remember only our farm, the McDouw's, and the boys' hostel bordering Ichicka Forest. I went there a few times with my father."

"Yes, the boys' hostel," he said quickly. "My mother was a caregiver there. We lived in a small house behind it. There were goats, chickens, and a big brown cow called Miss Daisy." He smiled.

We walked farther along the beach, the moon shimmering on the ocean, stars lighting our path. Our conversation flowed easily—from work to favorite foods, to everyday little things. Normal things. Peaceful.

"It's getting late," I murmured as we reached my car. "Thank you for the lovely evening. It was... a welcome distraction. But I should get some sleep. I need to dive into research tomorrow—about the wolves."

I turned to him, meaning to say goodnight. But then his eyes locked on mine, and before I could think or stop it, he leaned in—gently pulling me closer.

His lips brushed mine, tentative at first. A question. A plea.

My heart thundered in my chest. My skin tingled with electricity. The kiss was soft but intense, a slow build of something aching and new. I didn't pull away. I leaned into him, my hands finding his arms for balance—for connection. No one had ever kissed me like this. Like I mattered. Like something forgotten was being remembered.

His touch lingered... and then he pulled back.

"Goodnight, my sweet Gaea," he said, his voice low, eyes still locked on mine. "I hope you sleep well. And that we can do this again."

All I could manage was a breathless, "Uh-huh." My cheeks burned. My lips still tingled. I got into my car, and the drive home blurred past in a haze. The kiss had stirred something in me I thought I'd buried with my grief—something warm, alive, and terrifying.

Something I wasn't ready to name.

****

Cador

Her scent still clings to me—sea salt and something wild. Her body pressed against mine like it belonged there. Like maybe the space between us had always been wrong. Like it had always been meant to close.

I didn't expect it to hit me like that.

Not just the kiss—but the way she leaned into me. No hesitation. No fear. Just trust and breath and that quiet sigh she let out halfway through…

That sigh. I felt it everywhere. Like it wasn't just a sound but something that slipped under my skin and carved out a space for her in my bones.

And the way she looked at me—like she was handing me something fragile and dangerous all at once. Like if I didn't take that kiss, I'd lose something I didn't even know I needed.

But now I know.

I need her.

Not in some shallow, possessive way. Not just for the way she felt in my arms—though that's branded into me now. But for the way her presence slows the world down. The way her voice softens the edges of everything. That kiss made the rest of the world vanish. For a moment, there was only her.

And now… I want more.

No. I *need* more.

More of her. More of those moments. More of whatever that kiss unlocked inside me. She kissed me like she meant it. Like maybe… she'd been waiting for it too.

And now? I don't think I can go back to pretending.

CHAPTER TWENTY

Back in her apartment, Gaea's fingers drifted to her lips, still tingling from Cador's kiss.

What just happened?

I kissed him.

Or maybe *he* kissed *me*. I don't even know—does it matter?
All I know is, the second our lips met, something inside me cracked open.

I've spent my whole life being careful. Careful not to need too much. Careful not to lean on anyone. Because when the people who are supposed to stay—the ones who tuck you in and promise to come back—don't, you learn not to get used to anything too good.

But he felt *good*.

He felt... *safe*.

And when he held me—his hand warm and steady at my waist—I didn't flinch. I didn't shrink. I leaned in.

What does that mean?

I've never done this before. Not even close. I don't know how to be someone's *anything*. But in that moment—just that one beautiful, terrifying, soul-splitting moment—I didn't feel broken or afraid.

I felt *wanted*.

He kissed me like I mattered. Like I was something soft in a world that's spent years trying to harden me.

And the truth is… I want more.

I *still* want more.

But that terrifies me.

Because needing someone? Letting them in? That's how you get hurt. That's how you lose pieces of yourself you don't always get back.

Still…

When I stood there with him, the waves whispering behind us, the night wrapped around our shoulders like a secret—I didn't feel small. I didn't feel alone.

I felt *seen*.

And I can't stop thinking about the way he looked at me afterward. Like he knew. Like he *felt* it too.

I don't know where this goes. I don't know how to be someone's person.

But I want to try.

Even if it scares me.

Especially because it scares me.

A strange cocktail of warmth and vulnerability settled in her chest. But beneath it all, a persistent unease flickered like a storm just beyond the horizon.

She stood and began to pace, her bare feet silent against the wooden floor. Her gaze landed on the stack of her father's journals—worn leather covers filled with notes, sketches, theories. The history of her family. The mystery of the wolves.

But tonight, none of it held her attention.

Not fully.

Her mind was still on *him*.

Cador.

The way his voice faltered when she asked about Graceway. The way his tone shifted when he mentioned the boys' hostel.

It hadn't seemed like a lie. Not exactly. But it hadn't felt like the *whole* truth either.

She crossed the room, picked up her phone, and pulled up a search bar. Her fingers flew across the screen.

Boys' hostel near Ichicka Forest. Graceway. Caregiver staff.

Residential housing.

The results loaded slowly, the silence stretching thin around her.

Nothing.

No records of a caregiver named Cador's mother. No mention of a family living in a house behind the hostel. No goats. No chickens. No cow named Miss Daisy.

It was like that part of his life had been erased—wiped clean.

Or hidden.

Her throat tightened.

Who *are* you, Cador?

And why do I still want you, even when part of me is screaming to be careful?

CHAPTER TWENTY-ONE

A dreamless night.

I woke with a dry mouth and an insistent need for coffee. Downstairs, I brewed a strong cup, grabbed an apple, and leaned against the counter as the first sip burned comfortingly down my throat. My mind betrayed me with *his* memory—Cador's kiss. His soft lips. His arms, strong and steady. A strange warmth bloomed in my chest.
What is this feeling?

I wanted to linger in it. To imagine his arms around me again.

No. Focus.

The wolf. The research. The envelope.

I rushed upstairs and threw on a pair of shorts and a T-shirt. My study—the converted spare bedroom—waited. Journals from Mamo and Papo stacked like little secrets. And there, untouched for weeks, sat the yellow envelope.

Today. I couldn't put it off any longer.

It smelled of old paper and something faintly sweet—like time and dust and things forgotten. My fingers hesitated before peeling back the seal. Inside was a single letter, folded carefully.

I pulled it out and began to read.

"My darling daughter, if you are reading this, it means that we are gone and were unable to explain your legacy."

My heart lurched.

Legacy?

"You are born from a strong, gifted bloodline—the Angevins. Our secrets, our burdens, hidden from you for your safety… and for humanity's. Everything is explained in this letter."

My breath caught.

"Ichicka Forest—all 4.5 million acres—is yours. A burden, I know. But please… read on."

I stared at the page, disbelieving. My hands trembled.

"Ichicka is not a normal forest. It is magical… and dangerous. Its plants heal beyond modern medicine. Its animals guard ancient secrets."
"Your ancestor, Cormac Angevin, founded Graceway. He came to destroy a mystical evil known as Achlys—the dark one. She plagued the forest, slaughtering humans and beasts alike. But Cormac had a gift—he could commune with nature… and with the shapeshifters who dwell deep within Ichicka. Wolf-like beings, born of magic."

Shapeshifters?

"Cormac and Amena, the matriarch and firstborn of the shapeshifters, made a pact. A descendant from each side, bound by love, would one day drive Achlys into the abyss and destroy her forever."

"Achlys learned of the pact. And vowed: if the destined lovers failed to wed under the purple moon, she would break free—consuming souls and ruling the ruins of the world."

I blinked.

Purple moon?

"Cormac created a mixture—shapeshifter blood, cherrywood, lady's bedstraw, fern lily. He smeared it across the four corners of Ichicka closest to Graceway, holding her back. Every thirty years, the seal must be renewed. If not, Achlys can move through the forest freely, spreading destruction wherever she goes."

I couldn't breathe.

"My beautiful daughter, we believe this curse—or blessing—falls to you. Only a few know the truth. Be wise. Be brave."

"Love, Papo."

I sank into the desk chair, stunned.

A purple moon? A blood pact? A witch?

This couldn't be real.

I reached back into the envelope and pulled out two more papers—a detailed map of Ichicka, four sites marked in red, and a recipe for the sealing mixture. Everything was carefully drawn, labeled in Papo's neat script.

I stared at them.

"I own a magic forest with talking wolves and an ancient evil witch?" I muttered to myself. "They weren't crazy…"

I looked to the stack of journals.

Maybe they'll explain more.

I hesitated… then added with a nervous laugh, "Well, no need to worry about me falling for one of those magical creatures. I already met a nice, normal guy in Wave Crest."

The laughter echoed a little too sharply in the quiet room.

Still holding the map, I reached for the first journal box.

CHAPTER TWENTY-TWO

The day dissolved into a blur of faded ink and detailed sketches. Papo's journals were meticulous, filled with observations on local farm animals, treatments, and remedies. But nothing about the wolves, nothing about their strange affliction.

My phone's sudden ring startled me. It was late afternoon, the sunlight slanting through the study window.

"Hey," Cador's deep voice filled my ear. "Dinner and a movie?"

My heart skipped a beat. "Hi, Cador. I'm not in the mood for crowds, can we skip the movie?"

"Yes, I have the perfect spot I can take you, no crowds, I promise. I'll pick you up in an hour. Pepe's?"

"How did you know?" I asked, surprised.

He chuckled. "Delivery orders. Logical deduction."

I giggled. "I'll be ready."

A flurry of nervous energy filled me. What to wear? Why do I even care? I scolded myself, but my hands settled on tight blue denim, a lace-trimmed shirt, and white sandals with sparkling details. He's always seen me a mess.

The shower was a brief escape, coconut shampoo, lavender-almond oil body wash, the familiar scents of Mamo's recipes. Even my toothpaste was all-natural, from the health deli down the road.

As I slipped on my sandals, I heard the gate open. Butterflies fluttered in my stomach. I rushed downstairs, a smile already forming.

"Hi—" The word died in my throat. It wasn't Cador. It was Daddo, his eyes red and swollen, his face pale.

"Daddo? What's wrong? Where's Grammy?" I asked, my voice tight with worry.

"My darling girl," he choked out, his voice thick with tears. "I tried to call… It's Grammy. She had a stroke and didn't make it to the hospital."

"She was fine," Daddo sobbed, his voice ragged, "and then… nothing. I don't understand."

A gasp escaped me, a raw, broken sound. I wrapped my arms around him, tears streaming down my face. Daddo's frail legs buckled, and we sank to the floor, a tangle of grief.

"She was my life," he cried, his voice thick with pain. "Everything. Why did she leave me? She was the strong one."

I tried to compose myself, to lift him, but my own tears blurred my vision. Just then, the gate creaked open, and a figure moved into the light.

Cador. He lifted Daddo as if he weighed nothing, his strength a stark contrast to Daddo's fragility. My eyes widened in surprise.

"Where can I put him?" he asked softly, his voice a gentle rumble. "He needs to rest."

"Upstairs," I stammered, my voice thick with tears. "First door on the left. I'll make him some chamomile tea to calm him."

I brought the tea, my hands shaking. Daddo looked up at Cador, his eyes filled with unspeakable sorrow.

"Please," he whispered, his voice barely audible. "Keep my granddaughter safe. She's had too much… tragedy."

"I promise you, sir," Cador said, his voice firm, "I will protect her with all my being."

I gave Daddo the tea. "Drink this, Daddo. It will help you sleep. You can stay here tonight. We'll figure things out in the morning." I could hear his muffled sobs as we left the room.

"Thank you, Cador," I said, my voice barely a whisper. "I'm so sorry, about tonight."

He stroked my hair, tucking a stray strand behind my ear. "Don't apologize. I'm here for you."

"I'd… I'd like that," I said, tears welling up again.

We sat on the couch, the silence heavy with grief. I rested my head on his lap, and he gently stroked my hair, his touch a soothing balm against my pain. I cried until I had no more tears left, and then, exhausted, I drifted into a fitful sleep.

"I will stay as long as you need me, my sweet Gaea," he whispered, his voice a low, comforting murmur.

CHAPTER TWENTY-THREE

Two weeks had passed since Grammy's funeral.

Daddo was fading.

The doctors said it was Alzheimer's, likely triggered by the shock. He and Grammy had moved into a retirement village a year after I left home—insisting they didn't want to be a burden. Now, he was in frail care. Now, he was losing her twice: first her physical presence, and now the memory of her.

"Thank you," I whispered to Cador as we parked outside the WC Frail Care Facility. The building loomed, quiet and unassuming beneath a gray sky. "For being here. I don't know how I'd manage alone."

He leaned over and pressed a kiss to my cheek. "I've fallen so hard for you, Gaea," he murmured, voice thick with emotion. "I'd move mountains if you asked me to."

Tears welled in my eyes—grief mixing with something I couldn't name. Something deeper. Warmer. More dangerous.

"Don't cry, love," he said gently. "Do you want me to come in with you?"

"No." My voice cracked. "I need to see him alone. He doesn't remember me... and I don't want you to see that pain."

His eyes darkened, a shadow of hurt flickering across his face. "Very well," he said quietly. "I'll wait here."

The sterile scent of disinfectant slapped me the moment I stepped inside. The receptionist barely glanced up as I signed in. Carpeted corridors muffled my footsteps. I moved on instinct—like walking into a dream you didn't want to remember.

Room 102.

I paused outside the door, gathering my breath, then stepped in.

"Oh, what a pretty girl you are," Daddo said, eyes unfocused, voice bright.

I leaned down and kissed his forehead. "Hi, Daddo. How are you feeling?"

"Great, thanks. Waiting for my Jello," he giggled, turning toward the window like a child.

The room was small and cold, scrubbed clean of personality. A hospital cot, a steel dresser, a plastic water jug. No photos. No books. Just Daddo, adrift in a fog he couldn't see through.

We sat in silence for a while—him smiling at the trees beyond the window, me watching him. Thirty minutes later, a young man wheeled in a dinner trolley.

"Hi, Jerry. Dinner time," he said warmly.

"Jello?" Daddo clapped his hands, eyes bright.

"Yes, Jerry—but dinner first," the aide said patiently.

I stood. "How is he?" I asked gently.

"I'm sorry, miss," the young man said. "I just make sure he eats. You'll need to speak with Sister Galavan for anything else."

"Thank you, Lance. I appreciate it."

I bent and kissed Daddo's forehead again. "See you soon, old man."

But he was already absorbed in his meal.

Sister Galavan sat at her desk, flipping through a clipboard. She was stout, with silver hair and old-fashioned glasses perched low on her nose.

"Yes, dear?" she asked as I approached.

"I'm checking on Jerry. Room 102."

She gave a slow, measured nod. "He's… comfortable," she said, her voice professional, but not cold. "Some days are good. Some are less so. Alzheimer's is an unforgiving disease. Not curable."

Her tone shifted, softer now. "He's currently in the second stage— memory loss, wandering, anxiety. The final stage… it varies. Could be months. Sometimes years. But in the end, it's not pretty."

She paused, studying me. "You're his granddaughter?"

"His only living relative."

"I'll keep you informed if anything changes," she said gently.

"Thank you," I murmured, blinking fast against the tears burning behind my eyes.

Outside, Cador stood by his truck, hands in his pockets. The sight of him—solid, waiting—was a balm.

"How is he?" he asked, voice low and full of concern.

"As good as he can be," I said, my voice trembling. "The nurse told me what to expect…" I couldn't finish. The words crumbled, and tears spilled.

He pulled me into his arms without hesitation. Strong and warm, he held me together while everything else fell apart.

"Come," he said softly. "Let me take you to my secret place. We'll get dinner. You need air. And peace."

He opened the truck door for me like a silent promise—a promise of comfort, and maybe, just maybe, something more.

CHAPTER TWENTY-FOUR

The drive stretched on, darkness swallowing the landscape. The truck's headlights illuminated only the winding dirt road ahead, climbing steadily into the unknown. About an hour outside of town, a prickle of unease settled in my gut.

"You're not planning to dump my body in a field or something, are you?" I asked, a nervous laugh escaping me.

"Hahaha, no, silly," Cador chuckled, his voice warm and easy. "Just a little further. I promise—it'll all make sense."

At the summit, a string of fairy lights twinkled, illuminating a small food truck. A hand-painted sign proclaimed: **Fred's in Dredd's**. But the real magic wasn't the truck. It was the view—an endless, dark expanse where the city lights kissed the ocean, a sea of glittering stars above and below. I gasped, my breath stolen by the beauty.

"Here we are," he said as the truck came to a stop.

Fred, a Jamaican man with thick dreadlocks and a gentle smile, greeted us with the smell of roasted coffee and something sweet.

"Anything specific you'd like?" he asked me.

"No, surprise me," I giggled.

"Hi Fred. Two 'Double Jar Specials' and a 'Swing for Two,' please," Cador said.

"Coming right up!" Fred answered.

He handed us a massive Kahlua-infused chocolate milkshake dusted with hazelnut sprinkles, and a shareable basket of crinkle-cut fries, spicy wings, riblets, and mini cheese grillers.

We settled at a secluded table, the aroma of spiced wings and sweet coffee thick in the cool night air. The moonless sky amplified the stars, casting everything in a gentle, silver glow. It felt almost sacred.

"It's stunning up here. I never knew this place existed," I whispered.

"Not many people do," Cador said, smiling. "It's mostly runners, hikers, and mountain bikers who know about Fred and this place."

Suddenly, Cador's posture stiffened. The hair on his neck rose, his body subtly shifting. His expression darkened for a flicker of a second.

"What's wrong?" I asked, instinctively reaching for his hand. "Are you okay?"

He softened, forcing a smile. "Just... thought I heard something in the dark."

"There aren't any dangerous animals in Wave Crest," I reassured him. "And the stray wolves never come this far."

But his wolf senses picked up something—someone—lurking just beyond sight. Young. Omega, maybe. Clever boy, he thought. Keeping just out of range.

"This Kahlua is delicious," I said, giggling as I took a long sip. "Is there alcohol in this? I don't usually drink."

"I'm sorry," Cador said, his voice laced with concern. "I should've asked first."

"No, it's great."

But soon, my head began to spin. My legs felt heavy, my thoughts foggy. *Ooh... why am I so dizzy?* The "Double Jar Special" had an extra shot of dark rum—a detail Cador, with his shapeshifter tolerance, had overlooked.

"I really am sorry," he said, watching me closely. "Let me take you home."

"Home, shmome," I slurred, already drifting off as he buckled me in.

****

At my house, Cador carried me to my room, gently removed my shoes, and tucked me under the blanket. He leaned down and kissed my forehead.

"Sleep tight, my precious one," he whispered.

As he turned to leave, I stirred and caught his hand. My voice was barely above a whisper. "Please... don't leave me. I don't want to be alone. Stay."

"I will stay," he said, voice a deep, steady rumble.

He settled in the corner, watching over me like a silent guardian.

****

A sudden clatter from downstairs jolted Cador awake.

"Gaea!" he blurted, bolting upright. He'd fallen asleep.

He found me in the kitchen, dancing with headphones on, barefoot, my T-shirt slipping off one shoulder. His gaze lingered on my legs, a smile tugging at his lips. The aroma of frying bacon and brewed coffee filled the air.

The toaster popped, and he flinched. I spun around, nearly hurling the spatula at him.

"You're up!" I beamed. "I made breakfast. To thank you." I poured him a cup of coffee. "Sugar? Cream?"

"Black," he said, his voice still rough with sleep. "Strong."

"I had a great time last night," I said with a grin. "But I think I'll pass on the Fred Special next time."

"I'm glad you had fun. I... I have to go," he said, regret flickering across his face. "The plantation at the sanctuary needs checking."

My smile faltered. "But... breakfast?"

"Rain check? I'm sorry. If the irrigation fails, the crops will wither."

"Fine," I sighed, packing the food into a container. "You can have breakfast for lunch."

I walked him to the front door. He pulled me into a long, lingering kiss.

"I wish I could spend the whole day with you," he murmured.

"Me too," I whispered back.

"Bye."

"Bye."

***

My knees weakened as I closed the door behind him. *How did this happen?* From wanting him gone... to wanting him to stay. A soft ache bloomed in my chest. *Wake up, Gaea. There's a wolf to save. And journals to read.*

After eating alone and cleaning up, I returned to the study with a sigh. The next box was heavier than the others, sealed with thick tape. I found the scissors and popped the lid open.

Inside was a piece of snow-white wolf fur. My breath caught. I touched it gently. It smelled like pine and wind and something ancient. There were two journals labeled **Discoveries**, and a leather-bound book— old, almost ancient. A smaller box was marked: **Blood and Skin Samples**. Papo's samples from Ichicka. I remembered his meeting with Mayor Stein. He'd said he needed to talk about something important.

I opened the old book. The scent of pressed flowers and vanilla filled the room. The title read:

Cormac Angevin: My Accounts of Ichicka Forest and the Promise of Our Bloodline

The story Papo told us while camping...

My chest tightened with memory and loss. I flipped through the pages, dismissing the first as folklore—until I stumbled across something that made me pause.

Achlys, cursed to roam the dark muddy pits of Ichicka, a panther-shifter, beautiful and deadly, destroying all who entered. In human form, stunning—yet twisted by hunger for power. She seeks freedom to rule the earth.

Amena, her twin, a white wolf-shifter. Born of the forest's light. Protector of her pack, the land, and the nearby humans. She was not bound like Achlys and could grow her bloodline.

Twin daughters of the forest's magic—equal in beauty, opposite in purpose.

A pact was made between the Angevin family and Amena's bloodline: the tenth generation—a human girl and a shapeshifter—would wed under the purple moon, finally banishing Achlys forever.

But a curse was etched into the pact: should they fall in love and one die unnaturally while the other bears witness... Achlys will break free from her prison.

I scoffed. "Ridiculous." Just folklore. Vivid imagination, nothing more. But...

The white wolf fur. A gift from Amena's pack?

I turned another page. A family tree.

Later, I thought, setting the book aside, heart pounding.

First, *the* *journals.*

CHAPTER TWENTY-FIVE

Later that day, I packed the blood and skin samples along with the "Discoveries" journals into my backpack. It was late Sunday afternoon, but the shelter stayed open until 8 p.m. I needed answers—now.

Grabbing my keys, I stormed out the front door and drove across town. The lot outside the shelter was empty when I pulled in, an eerie quiet settling around the building like a shroud.

Inside, only two voices echoed softly—Mindy, the weekend receptionist, and Nicky, a veterinary intern. They sat at the front desk, speaking in hushed tones.

"Hey, ladies," I said, rushing past them. "Just checking on some samples." I didn't wait for a response as I hurried into the lab and began unpacking the contents of my bag.

The samples were meticulously labeled:

- **Wolf A** – Healthy Male

- **Wolf B** – Healthy Female

- **Wolf C** – Infected Male

- **Wolf D** – Infected Female

I started with the first journal, the one documenting the female subjects.

Subject B:
Young female, no external exposure.
Bloodwork normal.
Strong vitals.
Glossy fur. Pink tongue. Clean teeth.
Returned to Ichicka.

Subject D:
Found near Graceway.
Bloodwork abnormal.
Parasite-like virus attacking white blood cells.
Irregular vitals.
Matted fur. Ticks. Pale tongue. Rotting teeth.
Quarantined.

Three-Month Follow-Up

Subject B: Paired with a Beta male.

Subject D: Deceased.

****

Next, I opened the journal on the male wolves.

Subject A:
Young Beta male.
No outside exposure.
Healthy bloodwork.
Strong vitals.
Glossy fur. Pink tongue. Clean teeth.
Returned to Ichicka.

Subject C:
Lone male found near the Angevin farm.
Bloodwork highly irregular.
Virus observed to be controlling—not mutating—cells.
Vitals erratic.
Predatory speed.
Matted fur. Bald patches. No ticks/fleas.
Pale tongue with black line. Breath foul.
Quarantined.

Three-Month Follow-Up

Subject A:
Paired.
Offspring expected.

Subject C:
Escalated symptoms—blackened eyes, white foam, extreme aggression.
Declared dangerous.
Untreatable.
Attacked Dr. Manahan.
Euthanized

Outcome:

Subject C – Terminated

Peter Angevin

****

My breath caught. A chill climbed my spine.

Could this be the same infection affecting the wolf at the sanctuary?

I placed one of the slides under the microscope. But these samples were old—and the red blood cells… different. A sigh slipped from my lips. I hadn't been back to the sanctuary in over a month.

The last time I was there, Lizzy and I were at the zoo for the annual animal check-ups.

I let out a nervous laugh. Cador won't mind me coming by to take a blood sample... and maybe steal a kiss, too.

I packed my things again and headed for the sanctuary.

CHAPTER TWENTY-SIX

The sanctuary was more than just a refuge—it was a legacy. Owned and run by the Whelan pack, Cador's bloodline had protected it for generations. Beyond serving as a haven for shapeshifters, it doubled as a hub for agricultural studies, livestock research, and conservation programs. It was also a safe harbor for their youth, a place to stay while attending WC University before returning to Ichicka.

Deep within the woods, hidden from human eyes, lay their true village—a place where shapeshifters could live freely. Some stayed in human form, raising families with spouses who could never shift. Others ran wild beneath the moonlight. Warriors often chose strong, unmated wolves to breed powerful offspring. Farmers and kin-bound wolves, however, chose human mates, ensuring the survival of their community's softer, essential roles.

"How is he?" Cador called out as he strode across the sanctuary's gravel path, voice sharp with tension.

"He hasn't eaten," Damean, his second-in-command, replied. "But he's strong. Pacing. Sniffing the air like he's... waiting."

"We need a blood sample," Cador said, his tone firm.

Damean furrowed his brow. "Why? Didn't you say Lizzy's girl would be coming soon?"

"No!" Cador snapped. "I don't want her anywhere near him. Something's off. He's not like the others we've found—there's something wrong with this one. Tranquilize him. I'll get the sample myself."

Damean loaded the tranquilizer gun and fired. The dart hit, but the wolf barely flinched. Its knees bent slightly, but it remained standing—defiant, glaring.

"Another," Cador commanded.

Damean hesitated, then fired again. The wolf staggered but didn't fall.

"Again."

"That'll kill him," Damean warned. "And it'll raise questions with the girl."

Cador paused, eyes narrowing. "Any civilians on the property?"

"None. Just us."

"Lock the doors. No interruptions," Cador ordered, already stripping off his shirt and jeans.

Damean moved quickly, bolting the front gates and securing the interior doors.

Cador stood bare and imposing, eyes locked on the agitated wolf.

"Listen, wolf," he muttered, voice low and primal. "I don't like changing here. But if you won't submit to me as a man, then you'll bow to me as Alpha."

Damean returned just as the shift began—bones cracking, flesh stretching, the familiar, brutal beauty of transformation. Cador's frame expanded, his jaw elongating into a snarl as black fur rippled down his spine. Even restrained, his form was awe-inspiring.

The wolf tensed, but when Cador drew closer, it finally rolled onto its back—submitting.

Take the blood, Cador commanded telepathically.

Damean hurried forward, drew the sample, and retreated with a slight shudder. *There's something not right about him.*

Cador tried to connect—mentally, spiritually. But there was nothing. A block. Cold and impenetrable.

Who are you? he wondered. *And why do you feel so… wrong?*

Damean returned, vial in hand. "Got it. I'll store it in the sample fridge—"

The sound of a car pulling up cut him off.

"Hello? Anyone here? Cador?" Gaea's voice rang through the sanctuary.

Cador's heart sank. *Why now?*

"Quick," he growled. "Put the sample away. Keep her busy. I'll change back."

Damean nodded and rushed off. *Silly girl,* he thought. *Always chasing wolves.*

****

"Hi! Gaea, right?" Damean said, opening the door with a bright smile. "I'm Damean. I work with Cador."

"I remember. I saw you the other day. Is Cador around?"

"He's out back. We were just—"

"Hey, love," Cador's deep voice interrupted. He emerged barefoot and shirtless, jeans hanging low on his hips. My breath caught in my throat at the sight of him—dark, rugged, and entirely too delicious for this early in the day. Damean took his cue and vanished into the office with a smirk.

"I came to get a blood sample."

"Thought you came to see me," Cador teased, trailing behind as I walked past him toward the kennels.

"That too," I admitted, biting back a grin. But I paused when I saw the scattered clothes on the floor. "Strip-teasing for the wolf now?"

Cador gave a sheepish laugh. "He was aggressive. We had to sedate him. Damean took the blood for you."

"I'm his doctor," I said flatly. "I should have taken the sample."

"We didn't want you getting hurt. It wasn't safe."

"So… you took off your shirt and shoes to help Damean get the blood?"

"Well… yeah. Didn't want to ruin my clothes," he said, scratching the back of his neck.

I narrowed my eyes. "Is Damean a vet?"

"No, but close enough. He's a human doctor."
"You're lucky you didn't hurt him. Our anatomies aren't the same."

Before I could say more, Cador stepped forward, grabbing my waist and kissing me—deep, hot, hungry.

I shoved him away, breathless. "Not fair. Was that to distract me?"

He grinned. "Did it work?"

"…Yes," I admitted, cheeks flushed.

"Come on," he said, reaching for a shirt. "Let's get you the right sample. No more surprises."

CHAPTER TWENTY-SEVEN

We walked through the sanctuary's back door, the setting sun painting the sky in hues of orange and purple. A cool breeze carried the scent of freshly turned earth.

"It's going to rain tonight," Cador said, sniffing the air.

"Really?"

"Yes. I can smell it."

"Neat trick. I just smell dirt," I teased.

The student bungalows were clustered together—small, charming structures with thatched roofs. A larger bungalow stood apart, distant from the rest.

Must be the dining hall, I thought, surprised by its distance from the main building.

Lush green grass and vibrant flowers lined the walkways, filling the air with a mix of floral and earthy scents.

"Can we go to your place first?" I asked as we approached the large bungalow.

"This is my place," Cador laughed, a playful grin on his face.

"But… it's so big," I stammered. "I thought you were one of the staff members here."

"I am," he said, unlocking the door, "but I'm also the owner. It's been in my family for generations. We house students here, like a hostel. We provide scholarships, so they don't have to worry about accommodation or food. The rest is up to them."

The front door was carved from oak, adorned with wolves and trees. "It's beautiful," I murmured, running my hand over the smooth wood.

Inside, the bungalow was unexpectedly luxurious. A four-poster bed dominated the open space, with a hidden bathroom tucked behind it. White sofas draped with faux fur flanked a stone fireplace, and a sleek modern kitchen lined the far wall.

"Welcome to my… holiday home," Cador said. "Can I pour you something to drink? And will you please stay for dinner? I'm making pan-seared striploin, garlic mashed potatoes, and roasted vegetables. Sangiovese or cranberry juice?"

"You're a connoisseur of more than just steaks."

"Just enough to avoid boring meals," he replied, slipping on an apron. "We grow most of our food here. I rarely eat out, except for Fred's as a treat. He buys all his stock from us—and he has the best coffee too."

"I *am* kind of hungry," I admitted, my stomach rumbling.

We chatted and laughed while Cador cooked, sharing stories of Graceway and childhood memories. He spoke fondly of Ichicka and how he and his friends used to play there as pups.

"I've been meaning to ask," he said softly, glancing over his shoulder, "what do you remember about the night your parents disappeared?"

I felt a shadow cross my face. "Not much. The psychologist calls it selective memory loss caused by trauma. It was my 10th birthday. I remember presents, getting my own tent, going camping in Ichicka Forest, Mamo's stew, s'mores... and going to bed. Then, nothing. I woke up in the park days later."

"I'm so sorry," Cador said, his voice filled with genuine empathy. "Do you ever want to go back?"

"Sometimes," I admitted. "But then I remember Daddo needs me. I'm all the family he has left."

Cador changed the subject. "Ready?" he asked, grabbing a remote and taking my hand. Soft music filled the room as he pulled me closer. We began to sway to the gentle rhythm.

For a moment, my memories faded. I felt light, safe... complete. *Can this be... love? What if I lose him?*

As if sensing my thoughts, he gave me one last spin and pulled out my chair. The meal was exquisite. The steak melted in my mouth, and the creamy mashed potatoes dissolved with each bite. I wasn't usually a wine person, but the Sangiovese paired perfectly. The rain began to fall outside, tapping gently against the windows.

Cador changed the music to something slower, more romantic. He pulled me from my chair again, holding me so close I could feel his warmth. His earthy scent was intoxicating—I wanted more.

He kissed me.

The kiss wasn't rushed. It was deliberate, tender, yet full of passion. Then, without a word, he lifted me off the ground and carried me outside into the rain. A warm drizzle dusted our skin as the open door's light lit his strong, chiseled features.

"I love you," he blurted.

"I love you too," I whispered, my voice soft but certain.

The rain stopped, and I laughed. "I feel like Cinderella at the ball. I have to go."

"Stay?" he pleaded, brushing wet hair from my face.

"I can't. I have to pick up Siggy at 7 a.m."

"Please change into dry clothes before you leave. You can take some of mine."

I laughed. "They won't fit me anyway. I keep a clean set of clothes in my trunk."

"The bathroom's this way," Cador said, ushering me toward a door behind his bed. "I'll grab your clothes while you dry off."

The bathroom was stunning—elegant marble-like tiles, bronzed fixtures, and more space than my entire bedroom back home. I grabbed one of his pure cotton towels. It smelled of lavender and sunshine.

Cador returned quickly. "Are you decent?" he called from outside the door.

"Yeah," I said, stepping out with one of his towels wrapped around me. My bare legs peeked out as I dried my hair.
"Do you *really* have to go?" he asked, a playful grin tugging at his lips.

"Yes, early morning. Now give me my bag so I can get dressed, please."

I popped back into the bathroom and slipped into a pair of jeans and a blue t-shirt. When I emerged, I gave him a quick kiss on the cheek.

"I'll grab the blood sample and call you when I'm home," I said, patting his chest as I headed toward the door.

"Call me when you're *inside* and the doors are locked," he insisted.

"It's Wave Crest," I said, smiling.

"Still a big city," he replied, his voice tinged with protectiveness.

As I stepped out into the night, I felt his gaze follow me. I didn't dare turn around.

If I did, I knew he'd draw me back in.

CHAPTER TWENTY-EIGHT

The insistent buzz of the alarm shattered the quiet of morning. "Urgh," I groaned, swatting at the clock. My hand fumbled for the snooze button while my mind spun through the day's checklist.

I need to tell Siggy and Lizzy about the sanctuary's lab.

I grabbed my scrubs, jeans, and undergarments, tossing them into a backpack. "What to wear?" I muttered, scanning the closet. Jeans and a T-shirt for the drive, and an extra set of scrubs to make laundry easier.

A quick wash, hair twisted into a neat bun, and I was ready. I tucked the journals safely into the backpack, zipped it shut, and slung it over my shoulder.

A few minutes later, I knocked on Siggy's door. It creaked open to reveal her, hair a wild halo around her head, dressed in a bright pink gown and dinosaur-shaped slippers.

"Good morning, sunshine."

"Too cheerful," Siggy groaned, yawning. "Did you... you know?"

"Really?" I rolled my eyes. "You told me to pick you up at 7:00 AM, remember?"

"Sorry," she muttered, rubbing her eyes. "I forgot. I've got to pick up my car from the mechanic at ten. Then the office."

"I'm heading to the shelter and then the sanctuary."

"You need to name him," Siggy mumbled, already half-turned back toward bed. "'That wolf' is boring. Call him Bobby. Or Boris." he aused, then added, "Now, can I please go back to sleep? It's *seven*."

"Bye, Sigs. Talk later," I said, chuckling as I headed for the car.

****

"Hey, Lizzy?" I called as I stepped into the shelter.

"Back here!" she called from the lab.

I followed the voice and paused in the doorway. "What's this?" I asked, eyeing three neatly packed boxes labeled *Research*.

"Your research," Lizzy said, brushing a stray hair from her face. "Damean called this morning. Cador wants you working with the wolf *at* the sanctuary."

"And here I was, rehearsing how to ask if I could work from there," I laughed. "It'll be easier to monitor him on-site. Siggy says I should name him Boris or something."

Lizzy raised an eyebrow. "They *never* let outsiders use their workspace. Take advantage of it."

"I'm confused. You work there all the time."

"I go there to collect samples or animals," she explained. "I bring them back here, test, treat, then return them. No one's ever gotten full access to their lab before. You're moving up, girl," she said with a wink.

"You just want gossip about Cador," I teased.

"Obviously. All of it. Promise?"

"We *need* to get you a man," I giggled.

She chucked a pencil at me. "Go make me proud."

CHAPTER TWENTY-NINE

I pulled into the sanctuary at 8:30 a.m. The sky was still waking up, the air crisp and filled with the scent of dew-soaked grass. I was unloading the research boxes when Damean stepped outside.

"Hi, Gaea. Need a hand?" he asked, already moving to grab one.

"Yes, please. It's my research," I said, hefting a box toward him.

"Great. Follow me—you're all set up. Office space, lab workstation, new sample fridge…" Damean grinned. "All ready for your *monsters*."

"Thanks, that's great."

"Thank the boss," Damean added as we walked. "He made sure you've got everything you need."

Royal treatment, I thought, following him into the building.

A woman emerged from Damean's office—a striking figure with blue eyes and black hair streaked with white. She smiled warmly.

"Hi."

"Gaea, meet my fiancée, Dana," Damean said, blushing slightly. "High school sweethearts."

"He's a hopeless romantic," Dana teased, rolling her eyes affectionately.

We all laughed. I glanced around the space, but one name hovered on my mind.

"He's not here yet," Dana said knowingly, her smile widening.

"Who?" I asked, too quickly.

Dana chuckled. "Cador. He's with the students, fixing the irrigation system."

"It's *still* broken?"

"No," she smirked. "He breaks it—on purpose. Says it challenges them to think critically. He'll be back later."

"Cador's gifted," she added, her voice softening. "He's got a master's in agriculture, completed a full chef's course, and he's a black belt in martial arts. Plus, he owns businesses all over the world—wine farms, art galleries, a cruise ship, a few hotels. Yet somehow, he stays grounded. This sanctuary and the people here come first."

"I'm impressed," I admitted. "Is there anything he *can't* do?"

"Yes," Dana grinned. "He *can't* stop talking about you."

We both burst into laughter.

CHAPTER THIRTY

I finished setting up my workstation, running a hand over the desk—a silent declaration of readiness.

"Can I please see the wolf?" I asked, already moving toward the door. "I want to check his vitals."

"Let's get you settled first," Damean said gently, noticing my eagerness. "Manual labor starts tomorrow."

He must have caught the flicker of disappointment on my face.

"I'll take you," he added, "but it's too late for tranquilizers. He needs to eat, and sedation messes with his appetite. We'll observe him instead."

"You're right," I admitted, though I couldn't shake the restlessness building in my chest. "I'll just take a quick peek then."

As we approached the kennel, Cador appeared.

"Hey, love. How are you?" he asked, his voice quiet and comforting.

"I'm good. You smell… strong today."

He laughed—an unfiltered, genuine sound. "Sun and sweat," he said casually, though his scent was something more—musky, earthy… strangely magnetic.

"What's the plan?" he asked, stepping closer.

"Just doing a quick check on the wolf," I said, pushing the kennel door open.

Cador moved beside me, gently brushing my hair back before kissing my forehead. He held the door open for me, his touch lingering just a second too long.

The moment I stepped inside, the wolf snapped to attention.

Its posture went rigid. Blue eyes locked on mine.

It was like a jolt of electricity crackled through the air between us.

"Did you see that?" I asked, breathless, my voice filled with awe. The connection was instant, intense—thrilling and unsettling all at once.

"We saw," Damean and Cador said in unison, both their expressions darkening.

"Let's get something to eat," Cador said suddenly, his tone calm but laced with urgency. "We can celebrate."

"I'll just grab my bag. Shower first?"

"Sure, love. My bungalow," he replied, managing a smile that didn't quite reach his eyes.

****

Later…

As they walked away, Cador cast one last glance back at the wolf.

Its eyes followed them.

And for a brief, bone-deep moment… he swore it was grinning.

A shiver crept up his spine.

He leaned in close to Damean.

"Go in there," he whispered. "Find out what you can. I need to know why it reacts to her like that."

Unease coiled in his gut. He hadn't shaken it since that moment in the kennel.

I don't want to scare her, he thought. *But I need to tell her the truth… soon.*

Damean nodded, understanding the weight behind the words Cador hadn't said aloud.

"That was insane," he later muttered to Dana. "The wolf's reacting to Gaea."

He handed her a tranquilizer gun and a taser.

"You can't go in there," Dana said firmly. "It's not safe."

"He's not contagious," Damean replied. "He's been here three months. And Peter's journals—"

The wolf paced the back of the enclosure, its eyes never leaving the door.

"I have a bad feeling," Dana whispered. "He's waiting… for something. Or someone. And the way he reacted to Gaea? It chilled me."

"I agree," Damean said grimly. "We need to keep a close eye on her."

CHAPTER THIRTY-ONE

I skipped toward the bungalow, excitement buzzing through me like electricity. The sun dipped behind the horizon, casting golden light over the sanctuary. The air was calm, but I could sense Cador's unease lingering just beneath the surface.

"What an incredible day," I beamed, practically glowing. "I hope the next blood sample shows improvement in the wolf. If he's stable, maybe he can move to an outdoor kennel here at the sanctuary."

"I'm happy for you," Cador replied, his voice warm. "What do you fancy for dinner?"

"Not sure yet. Can we decide after I shower?"

"Of course, love," he said with a soft smile. "We can even have breakfast for dinner if you like. Your wish is my command."

I placed my backpack on the bed, my fingers brushing over his white, silky bedding. The fabric was impossibly soft beneath my hand.

I felt him step up behind me, his warmth wrapping around me. I inhaled the scent of him—raw earth, sun, and sweat. Cador gently moved a strand of hair behind my ear, his voice low against my skin.

"Egyptian cotton. One thousand thread count," he whispered, placing his hand over mine.

A spark ignited between us, his desire radiating through the slight touch. His arm slid around my waist, pulling me back against him.

His lips brushed my neck, feather-light but full of promise, sending a shiver down my spine. I turned to face him, and the hunger in his eyes stole my breath.

Our kiss deepened, slow but intense. His tongue danced with mine, and my body melted into his. I should pull away—my mind and body at war—but I didn't want to.

He lifted me effortlessly, my legs wrapping around his waist, the electricity between us almost unbearable. He carried me to the bathroom and gently set me down, his breath ragged.

"Enjoy your shower, my love," he said with a teasing smile, then turned and closed the door behind him.

I stood there in silence, leaning against the cool marble. "What just happened?" I whispered, a soft laugh escaping my lips. "Why does he tease me like this?"

As I undressed, my thoughts spun like leaves in a breeze. He's driving me insane. It's getting hard to focus on my work—or anything else.

I folded my clothes neatly, then turned on the water. The warm stream cascaded over me, washing away more than just the day's sweat. Compared to the pathetic trickle back in my apartment, this was paradise.

Time is flying. I yawned. *I hope we don't go far. I still have to drive home.*

I wrapped a towel around myself and began drying my hair, only to realize I'd left my clothes on the bed.

Maybe he planned this.

****

Meanwhile...

Cador prepared for the evening.

A perfect night for stargazing.

He packed a small picnic: pomegranate juice in elegant flute glasses, fresh berries, handmade crackers, cured meats, and a wedge of Pecorino Romano imported straight from his farm in Italy.

We share our produce with the pack in Ichicka Village.

They were just like any other town—only hidden from the world's chaos. They deserved the best, too.

But as he laid out the items, his thoughts drifted again—back to the wolf. Its stare kept replaying in his mind.

Something about that look... it wasn't instinct. It was awareness.
He shifted uncomfortably, thoughts spiraling into darker places. The sanctuary was a safe haven, yes—but not everyone in the outside

world lived as freely as Ichicka's shapeshifters.

Out there, it's pack life or isolation.

But no one was forced. Even lone wolves could return, if they vowed loyalty. The rules were more than tradition—they were built into their blood. Every pack needed an Alpha. Someone to protect the pack... and the humans among them.

He glanced out the window at the stars. The sound of the running shower pulled him back to the present.

I need to clean up too. I smell like a barn animal.

He grabbed a clean t-shirt, jeans, and a towel, then headed outside to the emergency shower—his go-to after wrangling livestock or trudging through mud.

The cold water sent a shock through him at first but quickly turned invigorating. He washed up quickly and returned to the bungalow.

And froze.

Gaea stood in front of the bed, wrapped in a towel, her skin glistening slightly. His breath caught. It took every ounce of control not to drag her into his arms again.

****

"Oops, my clothes," she giggled, clearly flustered. "Why is your hair wet?"

"Outdoor shower," he replied. "Emergency use only. I can't take you out smelling like a stable."

He grinned. "You can finish up in the bathroom. Unless...?"

"No, that's fine," she said quickly, her cheeks flushing as her eyes flicked down his chest. She snatched her clothes from the bed and slipped into the bathroom.

Ten minutes later, she emerged, looking radiant.

"Where are we going?" she asked, eyeing the blanket and picnic basket.

"I thought we'd take the UTV up to the ridge," he said, smiling. "Night picnic. The headlights and solar lanterns are strong, but once we're done eating, we can switch everything off and do a little stargazing."

"That sounds perfect," she said, linking her arm with his.

He held the basket and blanket in one hand, leading her out under the starry night.

CHAPTER THIRTY-TWO

I drove us deep into the sanctuary. The evening was warm, the stars bright above us, and a crescent moon cast a gentle silver glow across the treetops. I parked at a quiet, grassy clearing and unfolded the blanket, placing solar lights around it like tiny glowing sentinels. Then I unpacked the picnic basket.

"This is amazing," Gaea said, laughing as she sat down. "I can't wait to try the cheese and crackers."

I poured pomegranate juice into two glasses and handed her one.

"Cheers," I said.

She clinked her glass with mine. "Thank you for this. Nature like this reminds me of my childhood."

Her words struck a chord—but not the way she expected. My expression faltered. I couldn't keep the truth hidden any longer.

"I brought you here to talk," I said, my voice lower, more serious.

"Away from everyone else… I need to tell you something. Something real. Please, just let me finish before you react."

Her brows drew together, concern replacing her smile. "What's wrong?" she asked, placing her hand on my arm. "Can I help?"

"This is… difficult," I said, heart heavy. "The other night, I asked about your parents. There's a reason."

I saw her shift slightly, unease creeping in. Her heart pounded so loudly, my sensitive hearing picked it up clearly.

"I was there, Gaea… the day after your parents disappeared. We met then. You were just a child. I was the one who took you to safety— away from Achlys. My mother, Niamh, brought you food. And her second-in-command, Malik, returned you to town the next morning."

Her eyes widened. "I don't understand," she whispered. "You were *there*? Why didn't anyone come forward about this Achlys? Why don't I remember *any* of it—your mother, you, anything?"

"Because of Ichicka," I said gently. "The forest has a kind of magical force field. It hides certain memories—especially from those who haven't accepted their connection to it. It's a protection spell. Until you accept your fate, your past stays locked away."

She stared at me in disbelief.

"Forest people? Magic?" she repeated, incredulous. "Are you being serious right now? Because this is sounding like a *very* elaborate joke."

"Please, Gaea," I said, gently but urgently. "I know how it sounds. But the wolf stories—your father's journals—they're true. Our ancestors made a pact with the forest and each other to protect both species.

There's a family tree—your family kept it, of both humans and shifters. It's all there. Just read it."

Her lips parted in shock. "You really believe this?"

I met her gaze. "Achlys took my father too. She didn't want him and your father to finish the ritual. They were meant to mix their blood with forest plants and mark the four corners of Ichicka, sealing its power."

Her breath hitched. "My parents?"

"A few years later, on your tenth birthday, Niamh and your father, Peter, tried to complete it again. But they missed a corner… and that left the forest vulnerable. Achlys could move more freely after that."

I paused, searching her face, hoping for some glimmer of recognition. "Afterward, I kept coming to the forest's edge. For a year, I waited, but then your grandparents took you away. I thought I'd lost you forever."

I sat back, exhaling slowly. "Years later, I came to Wave Crest to study. When I saw you at Lizzy's, I didn't recognize you—but I was drawn to you immediately."

"Stop," she said, her voice trembling. "This is too much. I was lost and alone in that forest. There were *wolves*. Why would they have spared me?"

"Because we don't eat humans," I said calmly. "It's forbidden. It makes us unstable. Dangerous."

Her eyes narrowed. "*We*? Are you saying you think you're a *wolf*?"

"No," I said, shaking my head. "Not wolf. Not human. We're *shapeshifters*. In the forest, we choose our form. But outside of it, we stay in the form we picked—except for me. I'm different. I'm their

Alpha. Their leader."

I stood, removing my shoes and pulling off my shirt.

Gaea stared at me for a long moment... and then burst into uncontrollable laughter.

"Oh my God," she gasped between peals. "Is this supposed to be a *striptease*? You're serious? I'm done. Take me back. NOW."

CHAPTER THIRTY-THREE

Before I could say another word, Cador shifted before my eyes.

His denim shredded like tissue paper, and black fur rippled over his skin, glistening under the moonlight. He grew in size until he towered over me, an enormous creature carved from shadows and raw power. His amber eyes burned like fire, locking onto mine.

"Gaea." The voice echoed—not aloud, but inside my mind. *"This is the form you saw me in... the first time we met in the forest."*

My mind reeled, struggling to reconcile the man I had come to love with the magnificent, terrifying beast standing before me. A wave of disbelief—and something dangerously close to fear—washed over me as the impossible became real.

My knees buckled. The world tilted.

And then—darkness.

****

"What a dream…" I groaned, gripping my throbbing head as I sat up slowly.

The room came into focus—Cador's room. Panic flickered to life in my chest.

I froze, eyes scanning my surroundings. Everything felt off. I was alone. Confused. My limbs ached—especially my arms and knees, like I'd fallen hard.

How did I get here? Where is he? What happened? Did he drug me? No. That didn't feel right.

It took a few dazed minutes before the fragments started piecing themselves back together.

The picnic. His confession. The black fur. The towering body. *The wolf.* No… not a wolf.

Cador.

I squeezed my eyes shut. My breath caught in my throat.

He shifted. Right in front of me.

I checked the time: 6:00 AM.

The sanctuary would still be asleep. Quiet. Safe—for now. I had to leave.

Now.

I slipped from the bed, every movement cautious and deliberate. I found my bag and keys where someone had neatly placed them— maybe him. The familiar weight of them in my hands grounded me, but only barely.

I crept through the bungalow, then into the main sanctuary building. The stillness was suffocating, amplifying the storm in my mind.

I was drained—utterly emptied—not from lack of sleep, but from emotional collapse.

Shapeshifters. Magic forests. Ancient pacts.

The words circled in my mind like a fever dream. Ridiculous… and yet I'd *seen* it. I'd *felt* it.

The only thought left, the only instinct that made sense, was to run. To get home. To slip back into the comfort of ordinary things.

A hot bath. Epsom salts. Lavender.

A temporary escape from the impossible truth that had cracked my world wide open.

CHAPTER THIRTY-FOUR

Cador was awake, but a heavy silence had settled over the bungalow. He hadn't moved much—just waited, listened, and breathed through the ache in his chest.

He had told Dana and Damean to give Gaea space. She needed time—a buffer against the storm she'd just weathered.

Final exams. Her grandmother's death. Her grandfather's sudden illness. And now... this.

The truth. The betrayal. Him.

The weight of it pressed heavily on him. Every breath stung with the fear that he might've broken something between them beyond repair.

I'll check on her later, he thought. But the deeper ache inside him whispered that she might never want to see him again.

****

Before leaving the sanctuary, Damean had spotted Gaea standing in front of the kennel. She'd paused, her eyes fixed on something—or someone—within.

The old wooden door creaked quietly as she slipped inside.

There were security cameras in the kennel for monitoring the animals. Later, they would review the footage.

But for now, all anyone knew was that she had gone in. Alone.

The wolf lay curled in the far corner, still as death.

Or so it seemed.

****

Inside the Kennel

The wolf's energy pulsed in the stillness, a hum that vibrated through the air like an unsung melody.

He sensed her the moment she entered—her presence unmistakable. Her energy was like no other. It clung to her like a second skin, thick with emotion and ancient echoes.

Though his body remained motionless, his mind was alive with anticipation.

The time has come, he thought, his inner voice a deep, feral rumble.

Destiny draws near. I will have my revenge. And she—She will have her freedom.

Then, as if summoned by that silent vow, two shadowed figures emerged beside him.

They didn't speak with voices, but their message was clear, cutting through the air like ice.

"The mission begins tomorrow."

And just as quickly as they came—

They vanished.

CHAPTER THIRTY-FIVE

I dropped my bag on the dining table and went straight to the kitchen to make chamomile tea. The apple-like scent lingered in the air as I climbed the stairs, filling the space with a quiet comfort. I ran a hot bath, adding lavender salts, and soon the calming aroma mingled with the steam curling up from the water.

The world felt unreal, dreamlike. I slipped into the tub, letting the warmth seep into my bones as I took slow sips of tea. My thoughts swirled, loud and tangled.

None of this can be real And yet... it was. If I hadn't read it myself in Papo's journals, or in Cormac's diary, I might still have dismissed it all as delusion. But the accounts aligned—painfully and perfectly—with everything Cador said.

A long, shuddering sigh escaped from deep inside me. My heart didn't know what to feel. My mind couldn't grasp the truth.

This was too much.

Maybe I'll visit Daddo today. He always brings me comfort, even if he doesn't fully remember me. Seeing him is like breathing clean air—something steady, something real.

I leaned back, letting the water soothe my aching body and thoughts. For now, I pushed everything else—wolves, shapeshifters, rituals—far to the back of my mind.

****

Back at the Sanctuary

Cador had asked a few of the students to clean up the picnic site. Scavengers had gotten into the basket overnight—nothing salvageable. Still, it needed to be cleared before others wandered by.

In the lab, Damean and Dana sat with steaming mugs of coffee, watching the footage from the kennels.

"Have you called her yet?" Dana asked as Cador entered.

"Not yet," he replied, rubbing his forehead. "I'm giving her space. It's... a lot."

Dana hesitated, then said, "There's something you should know. Gaea left some of her father's journals and a diary on her desk. I read the one labeled *Cormac's Diary* last night."

Damean looked up sharply. "And? What did it say?"

Dana's voice lowered. "You both do realize who Peter Angevin was, right?"

"Of course," Damean said, frowning. "Gaea's father."

"Not just that. Don't you remember what happened sixteen years ago? The night we tried to sneak out and witness the smearing ritual?"

Cador stiffened. He remembered.

Dana continued, her voice tinged with unease. "Peter and Niamh were supposed to complete the ritual that night to renew the protection over the forest—thirty more years of safety."

"My father and Niamh were assigned to the South and East borders," she said. "Peter and Gaea's mother were meant to do the North and West. But Achlys intervened. They never finished."

She looked at Cador. "Before Milak took Gaea into town, I overheard him telling Niamh that Peter only managed to smear the North border before he was taken. The East was left unsealed."

Cador's eyes widened. "That left the forest exposed—Achlys could move more freely. She began corrupting omegas, offering them power they didn't understand."

"Exactly," Dana said. "That's how she spread. Through weakness and promises."

"But why didn't you say anything sooner?" Cador asked, frustration creeping into his voice.

Dana's voice softened. "I was thirteen. Niamh was our Matriarch.

And... I wasn't even sure what I heard. I thought I imagined it."

"None of us knew better back then," Damean added grimly.

Cador let out a sharp breath. "I need to check on Gaea. After that, we need to deal with that wolf. There's something off about him."

He turned and walked out before Dana could share the rest of what she had read.

****

Later That Morning

My phone rang just as I stepped out of my duplex. I answered without looking, assuming it was Lizzy.

"Hey, Liz—"

"Hi, Gaea. It's me," Cador said quickly. "Please don't hang up. I'm sorry. I should've told you sooner—I just... I was afraid. I never meant to break your trust."

My throat tightened. "My head's still spinning. I need time to process everything. I'm spending the day with my grandfather. I told Lizzy I needed a break. Let's talk in a day or two."

"Of course," he said softly. "I'll be here when you're ready. Damean will keep an eye on the wolf. I love you, Gaea."

I swallowed the lump in my throat. "Thanks, Cador. I love you too... but I really need time."

I ended the call.

The silence after was deafening.

I do love him. Deeply. But what does that even mean now?

There's too much to process. I need to get through today first.

CHAPTER THIRTY-SIX

Cador stared at his phone, the weight of doubt pressing down on him. *I hope this is not the end for us.*

Suddenly, a commotion erupted from the kennel, ripping him from his thoughts. His heart pounded as he rushed down the corridor, every step filled with mounting tension.

"What's going on?" he demanded as he burst through the door.

"The wolf!" Damean shouted, panic threading his voice. "He's shifting."

Cador's eyes locked on the unfolding scene. His breath caught. "This cannot be."

The creature before them twisted and contorted, caught between man and beast. His once-blue eyes were now the color of midnight—black and gleaming with an eerie light. Razor-sharp canines flashed as he bared his teeth. Standing nearly seven feet tall, he radiated an aura of raw power and fierce defiance.

"What happened to you?!" Damean gasped, his breath hitching, wide-eyed in disbelief. Awe and terror warred across his face.

"Nothing happened to me," the creature snarled, voice low and menacing. "I am one of the forgotten—an outcast, rejected by the pact for not being good enough. I was lost and alone… until she saved me. I have pledged my life to her, and I will set her free."

Cador's voice thundered, cutting through the charged silence. "What is your name, wolf?"

The creature shrank back slightly, voice trembling. "I am called Bedwyr the Unknown. She has chosen me."

"Chosen you for what?" Cador demanded. "Beware, wolf—you lack the strength to challenge an alpha. Who is 'she'? What is your purpose here?"

A chilling smile crept across Bedwyr's face. "She is Achlys," he hissed. "First, she will destroy the girl… then you. She will break free from Ichika. The prophecy will fail."

Cador staggered, his face paling as the weight of Bedwyr's words sank in. "Gaea," he whispered, dread thick in his throat. "This… this is why Niamh warned me to stay away from her. She's the tenth generation of the Angevin clan—the one foretold in the prophecy."

Bedwyr laughed then—a manic, echoing sound that filled the room with icy dread. "Not all of the forgotten remain in wolf form," he said, his laughter rising. "You'll see soon enough."

Cador spun on his heel, urgency driving him as he shouted, "Dana! Call Gaea. Now! Don't startle her—ask to meet for coffee or something. Keep her on the line! I'm on my way."

Without waiting for a reply, he grabbed his truck keys and bolted out of the sanctuary. His mind raced as he sped toward WC Frail Care.

I   need   to   make   sure   she's   safe.

CHAPTER THIRTY-SEVEN

"There you go, Daddo," I said gently, pushing his wheelchair into the garden. We strolled beneath the leafy lavender tree, its yellow blossoms swaying softly in the breeze. The warmth of the day wrapped around us, sunlight dancing through the branches in golden ribbons.

Daddo smiled, his childlike enthusiasm shining through. "This is nice. Thank you, young lady. Have you seen my Mandy? We're supposed to go on a date, you know. Soon, I'll ask her to marry me," he said with a twinkle in his eye.

My heart ached. He'd once been a strong, hardworking man. Now… reduced to this fragile version of himself, caught somewhere between memory and make-believe. I swallowed my emotions.

"I haven't seen her yet, Daddo," I replied softly.

We spent the morning together. Daddo recounted tales from his youth and the moment he knew Mandy was *the one*. I'd heard the stories a thousand times, but I listened as though for the first—because each time, the way he lit up when speaking of Grammy made me feel warm inside.

"Is it lunchtime yet?" Daddo asked cheerfully, breaking me from my thoughts. "I want my Jello!"

"It's almost time. Let's get you back to your room before they bring the food," I said, smiling, turning his wheelchair around.

As we made our way down the hall, my thoughts wandered—back to last night. To Cador. The pain of what he'd hidden from me still stung, but underneath that hurt was something deeper. Love. Real and consuming.

Daddo's love for Grammy... it was the same kind of deep devotion I felt for Cador. That hasn't changed. He's still the same person. I just need time to process everything. But another thought struck like lightning—Cormac's diary. The prophecy.

Was Cador and I's connection forged before we were even born? My heart pounded. I needed to speak with him. I needed clarity.

"Hey, Jer, did you enjoy your stroll in the garden?" Lance greeted us as we reached Daddo's room. "You're just in time for lunch. Today's special is a toasted ham and cheese sandwich and sweet tea."

"And Jello?" Daddo asked with a grin.

"Of course, Jerry. With custard, too," Lance chuckled. "Come on in so I can serve you."

"Hi, Lance. Nice to see you," I greeted with a polite smile. I leaned down and kissed Daddo's forehead. "Bye, Daddo. Enjoy your lunch. I love you."

He didn't reply—his attention was already on his tray—but that was okay. I'd gotten used to it.

The midday sun blinded me momentarily as I stepped outside. I'd parked under a tree at the far end of the lot to avoid the worst of the heat. Waves of shimmer rose from the blacktop as I reached into my jeans pocket for the keys.

Eight years with this car. Maybe it's time to upgrade—*with central locking*, I thought wryly, fumbling with the key.

"Excuse me, miss?"

The voice startled me. I turned.

A young woman stood nearby, maybe early twenties, with short black hair, blood-red lipstick, and a lollipop hanging lazily from her lips. She wore black skinny jeans and a white tank top, her expression unreadable.

"Sorry to bother you," she said. "I'm lost. Can you direct me to the university?"

"Sure," I said politely. "If you walk straight down the parking lot, then turn left, you'll see a diner with a red roof—"

"Parking lot, left, red diner? How do I even know it's a diner?" she interrupted, frowning. "What's it called? Can you show me?"

I hesitated. Something felt...off. But she looked genuinely confused.

"Okay, come on," I said, walking toward the edge of the lot. "It's just down there. You see, where the sign—"

Before I could finish, a strong arm clamped around my waist from behind.

The breath whooshed from my lungs. My feet left the ground. I tried to scream, to fight, but the grip was too strong. I kicked, thrashed—nothing. The stench of sweat and leather filled my nose.

"Watch it!" the girl snapped to someone out of view. "She wants her alive."

I caught a glimpse of the van as they dragged me toward it. My keys slipped from my hand, clattering to the asphalt near the open door.

Then everything went black.

****

Scene Break

Inside the van, three figures moved with chilling precision.

Johnny—the driver—was a short, bald human with a cartoonish villain look. A pencil-thin mustache twitched as he glanced in the rearview mirror.

Next to him sat Frank, a hulking shapeshifter built like a bodybuilder. His blue eyes were sharp and unreadable, his presence intimidating.

And in the back, Carmen—lollipop girl—leaned against the wall, smug and relaxed.

"Are we picking up Bedwyr?" Johnny asked, glancing at her.

"No," Carmen said sharply. "He's revealed himself by now. Too risky to bring him here. He'll meet us at the crossing. If he survives, she'll reward him once she's free."

Johnny shrugged and started the engine. The van sped away, heading toward Graceway.

"It's around an eighteen-hour drive with stops," he muttered. "We'll rest halfway. They won't catch up in time."

The lollipop clicked against Carmen's teeth as she smiled.

CHAPTER THIRTY-EIGHT

Cador's truck screeched to a halt next to Gaea's abandoned car. The acrid scent of burning rubber hung in the air. Her little red vehicle still stood beneath the shade of a tree at the far end of the parking lot—untouched, but far too quiet.

He leapt from the driver's seat, the door barely clicking shut behind him as he stalked toward the frail care center entrance. But just as his hand brushed the door handle, a familiar scent stopped him cold.

Fred's omega. Two others. And Gaea.

His senses sharpened, instincts howling. He turned on his heel, following the scent trail toward the edge of the lot. His stride was purposeful, every breath feeding the fire building inside his chest. The trail ended abruptly—no more footprints, no lingering presence.

They'd taken her in a vehicle. Right here.

A glint of silver caught his eye. He crouched down and picked it up—
Gaea's car key.

Reality hit him like a fist to the chest. She didn't leave willingly. She was taken.

Adrenaline surged. His heart roared like a war drum as he yanked his phone from his back pocket.

"Dana!" he barked. "Tell Damean to bring you to WC Frail Care. I'll explain when you get here. Hurry!"

His Alpha command allowed no space for hesitation.

Dana was already moving before he hung up. "Come on, D. Emergency at WC Frail. Cador says now."

Twenty minutes later, Damean's truck pulled up beside Cador. The tension in the air was suffocating.

Damean was first to speak. "What's going on? Is Gaea okay? Is she still inside?"

"She's gone," Cador growled, rage thickening his voice. "They took her. I smelled two humans and a shifter. The humans may not understand what they're part of—but this wasn't a random act. This was calculated."

Dana's eyes widened, her voice tight. "What's the plan?"

"Dana, take Gaea's car back to the sanctuary," Cador instructed. "I'm going to interrogate Bedwyr. He knows where they've taken her."

Dana nodded, and without another word, she climbed into Gaea's car and pulled away. Damean slid into the passenger seat of Cador's truck. The air inside felt heavier than stone, every passing second weighted with dread.

They reached the sanctuary just past 3:00 PM. As Cador pulled the truck to a stop, Damean turned to him with quiet warning.

"Be careful. Bedwyr might not be able to kill you, but in human form, he can still make you bleed."

"I know," Cador snapped, already yanking off his shirt.

Dana jogged around the truck, breathless. "You think he's going to mid-shift?" she asked Damean. "To match Bedwyr?"

"Yes," Damean said grimly. "But Cador's strength surpasses his. Bedwyr's a beta at best. There's no contest. Still... Cador's *furious*. This could get ugly."

Cador stormed into the sanctuary's main building, his anger a living entity radiating off him. He didn't bother removing his jeans—his body shifted mid-stride, shredding the denim as his transformation overtook him.

Mid-shift, Cador was a behemoth.

Nearly ten feet tall, his presence was primal and terrifying. The lower half of his body was pure wolf—thick with black fur, haunches like coiled steel. His upper body was power incarnate, every muscle defined, every movement fluid and dangerous. His arms ended in long, clawed fingers. His chest rose and fell with heavy, angry breaths. His lupine face gleamed under the sanctuary lights—fangs bared, glowing amber eyes lit with vengeance.

"**Bedwyr!**" he roared, the sound shaking the walls. "**Where is she?**"

The door to the kennels exploded off its hinges as Cador tore it free and hurled it aside like scrap wood.

Bedwyr shrank back, his own mid-shift form trembling. Submission rolled off him in waves as he looked up at the Alpha.

Cador seized him by the neck, lifting him effortlessly and slamming him against the concrete wall.

"For your sake," Cador growled, claws digging in, "**give me a reason not to rip you apart. Tell me where they took Gaea!**"

He dropped Bedwyr, letting the shifter crumple to the floor in a coughing, gasping heap.

Bedwyr's voice trembled. "I… I cannot fight you, Alpha. I wouldn't survive. I don't want to die."

"Then talk."

Bedwyr's eyes darted around like a cornered rat. "Achlys wants you to follow her. She *knew* you'd come. She's waiting… in the southern quadrant of Ichicka. Near the tar pits. The place where she was once banished. She's going to use your pain. She wants you to *see* it. See her drain Gaea's life the night before the purple moon."

Cador's jaw clenched, his claws flexing with rage.

Bedwyr kept talking, driven by fear. "The purple moon peaks the following night. That's when she'll take *your* life force. She needs both of you to complete the cycle. When she's done—Achlys will be free to reign. The Dark Queen will rise again."

Cador turned sharply. "**Damean!** I need you and Dana here. Guard the students. No one leaves, no one enters without your say."

Damean nodded, his face grim. "What about you?"

"I'm calling Milak. He'll gather the strongest warriors. We meet at the Angevin farm. Achlys might have more than just these three—humans or otherwise. Milak's team will protect the village."

Damean's gaze drifted to the trembling shifter on the floor. "And Bedwyr?"

"Double dose of elephant tranquilizer," Cador growled. "If he survives that and wakes up—he should run. Because after I finish with Achlys, I'll hunt him down."

He strode from the room, mid-shift form crackling with tension, until he reached the hallway and shifted back to human. He made a direct path to his bungalow, where he packed fast—clothes, cured meat, water, protein bars, field gear. Every second wasted could cost Gaea her life.

He returned to the front office a few minutes later, dressed and ready.

"You sure you don't want backup?" Damean asked, his voice low. Cador met his gaze. "I need you here. If something happens to me, you're next in line. The students need an Alpha, Damean."

"Then let me come," Dana said, stepping forward. "I can fight—"

"No," Cador said, smiling faintly despite the turmoil. "Damean needs you to keep his head out of the clouds."

He pulled them both into a quick, fierce embrace.

"I love you both," he murmured, then turned and left without another word.

His truck roared to life. Gravel spat behind him as he tore down the road.

I won't catch them before Graceway, he thought grimly, his grip tightening on the wheel. *But I won't be far behind. And when I get there, gods help them—because I won't.*

CHAPTER THIRTY-NINE

My head throbbed as I slowly regained consciousness.

"Urgh… what happened?" I muttered groggily, rubbing at my temples.

The rough carpet of the van pressed against my cheek. The acrid stench of bleach burned my nostrils, and a metallic tang coated my tongue, ushering in a creeping sense of dread. I was in trouble. The low hum of the engine vibrated through my body.

"Oh, the princess is awake," the girl in the passenger seat drawled, twirling a new lollipop between her lips. "Relax, dear. It'll all be over soon." Her smug words earned a round of laughter from the others.

I scanned the interior, calculating my options. I was at the far back. In front of me sat a bulky man. The driver focused on the road, while the girl leaned lazily against the passenger door. I needed to get out of here.

If I screamed, it might draw attention—but out here, on this deserted road, that was a gamble. My best chance? Leap forward, shove the girl out, and bolt through the passenger door. The driver wouldn't be able to stop me without wrecking the van. But the big guy... Frank. He sat just behind the driver. I wasn't sure if I could outrun him.

No time for doubt. I moved.

I vaulted over the seat, my body driven by instinct and years of wrestling stubborn animals. The sharp scent of cheap hairspray filled my nostrils as I grabbed the girl by the hair. She yelped, startled and in pain. Frank lunged, but I caught him with a solid kick to the face, splitting his lip. For a moment, I had the upper hand.

I reached for the door handle—freedom within my grasp.

But I was too slow.

Frank recovered, his iron grip closing around me like a vice. He yanked me backward. I struggled, kicked, scratched—but then I felt it: a sharp sting in my neck. My limbs went heavy. Darkness swept in, and the world faded to black.

****

"You were supposed to keep an eye on her!" Carmen screeched, glaring daggers at Frank. She turned to the mirror, fussing with her hair where I'd tangled it.

Frank's eyes narrowed. His voice came low and threatening. "Careful, little girl. Know your place. I don't take orders from you."

"Calm down, both of you," Johnny snapped from the driver's seat. "We're all on the same side. Achlys' promise extends to all of us. We just need to stick to the plan." He shot a warning glance at Frank through the rearview mirror.

"You drive for a while," Johnny said. "I'll tie her up so this doesn't happen again. We only have one dose left, and we'll need it when we get to Chrissy's Roadside Motel."

He pulled into a gas station. Carmen went inside for snacks and water while Frank switched seats. Johnny climbed into the back with me, a scowl tightening his face.

"I hope you're worth all the trouble you cause," he muttered, securing the ropes around my wrists.

When Carmen returned, they were back on the road.

"Cador's probably in pursuit by now," Johnny said, settling back in the front seat. "But we've got a four-hour lead. Chrissy's is only two hours away. We'll stop there and rest for the night. He'll have to rest too— he won't drive straight through."

By the time they reached Chrissy's Motel, the sky had dimmed into twilight. The place looked like it had crawled out of a bad movie. Nearly deserted, flickering neon lights, cracked pavement, and a sagging sign that read "VACANT" in red.

Carmen jumped out first, her heels clicking sharply against the asphalt. "I'll get us two rooms," she said, eyeing Frank. "You're bunking with Miss Feisty. Johnny and I will take the other."

The reception stank of stale bread and cigarette smoke. Half-closed blinds filtered in the dying daylight. A broken couch slumped in the corner beside a dusty plastic plant. A flickering TV buzzed quietly on the counter.

Behind the desk sat an old woman in curlers, a long, thin cigarette dangling from her lips. Her bloodshot eyes didn't budge from the screen.

"Evenin', dear. How can I help you?" she croaked.

"I need two rooms. Each with two single beds," Carmen said briskly.

The woman smirked, her gaze flicking to the van. "Rooms 17 and 19 should do. Or," she added with a sly grin, "you could share a double with the big guy in 18."

"Eew. No, thanks," Carmen replied, wrinkling her nose. "Just the two I asked for. I'll pay cash."

"Suit yourself, hon." The woman slid two keys across the counter. "Out by ten tomorrow. No funny business."

"Yeah, yeah," Carmen muttered, grabbing the keys and stalking back to the van.

She handed one to Johnny. "Move the van near 17 and 19. We don't need the old bat seeing us carry her in."

Johnny backed the van into the shadows. Carmen opened the door to Room 17, and Frank hauled me over his shoulder, laying me on the bed furthest from the door.

"See you in the morning," Carmen said as she turned to leave. "We check out by ten, but I want us gone by seven—just to be safe."

"No problem. I'm always up early," Frank replied, glancing once at me, unconscious and bound.

He closed the door behind him with a muttered warning to no one but himself.

"Stay far away from the door."

CHAPTER FORTY

Bedwyr's story was one of bitterness and betrayal—a dark path that led him straight into the clutches of Achlys.

His mother, a shapeshifter, died giving birth to his younger sister—a human. Bedwyr was only thirteen, and from the moment their mother's lifeless body was carried away, he blamed the infant for her death. That hatred festered like rot within him.

When his sister turned four, Bedwyr lured her away from the village under the guise of a game. She followed him eagerly, trusting him completely. But once they were deep in the woods, the game turned cruel. He shifted into his wolf form and began chasing her, nipping at her heels, her laughter turning to frightened cries.

He caught and released her again and again, clawing at her tiny limbs, biting into her fragile skin. Her screams echoed through the trees, but they only seemed to satisfy something twisted inside him.

Milak and Bridget, out patrolling the area, heard the cries. They arrived just in time to catch him in the act. Milak forced him to shift back and dragged him, naked and snarling, to the forest's edge. As acting Alpha, Milak exiled him from the Ichika without hesitation. Bridget, horrified, wrapped the wounded child in her cloak and carried her home. Despite their efforts, she succumbed to her injuries. Their father—already hollowed by the death of his mate—never recovered from the loss of his daughter. He died not long after.

Bedwyr was left with no pack, no family—only the bitter taste of rejection. He found shelter in the abandoned Angevin barn, surviving by stealing from nearby towns. As the seasons turned, so did his resolve. He remembered the old stories—legends of Achlys, whispered warnings of wolves who sought her out for power and revenge.

None had ever returned.

But Bedwyr didn't care.

At seventeen, consumed by rage, he left for the southernmost edge of the forest—beyond the barrier that kept their lands protected. The trees thickened, the air turned sour with damp earth and decay. Days passed. The underbrush thickened like claws. The stench of tar and sulfur clung to him, coating his lungs with every breath. Unseen creatures rustled around him, ever-watching, ever-hungry.

Exhausted and half-mad, he dropped to his knees and screamed into the shadows.

"Achlys! I am a willing vessel! Use me to destroy those who cast me out! I'll do whatever you command—just set me free to reign at your side!"

The darkness stirred.

A venomous voice slithered from the gloom. "You?" it hissed, mocking. "What could *you* possibly offer me, child?"

The stench of sulfur intensified. A massive panther emerged from the shadows—her fur dark as pitch, her blue eyes glowing with ancient fury. Achlys.

Bedwyr's voice trembled, but he stood tall. "I can go where you cannot. I've heard the whispers. The prophecy. The girl who will end everything. The townsfolk speak freely around me—they see me as nothing. I'll find her. I'll bring her to you."

Achlys studied him with a gaze sharp enough to flay skin. Then, she shifted—black fur melting into pale skin, her human form towering, elegant and terrifying. Her long obsidian hair spilled down her back like a veil. Without a word, she bit into her forearm, thick, black blood dripping into a hollowed stone bowl.

"Drink," she commanded, her voice like winter steel. "If you survive it, you will carry a sliver of my power."

He took the bowl, his hands shaking.

"Sixteen autumns from now," she continued, "bring me the Angevin girl the night before the full purple moon. Make sure she and the Alpha of Amena's pack are in love—and that the bond is real. He will prove it by revealing his true form to her."

Bedwyr raised the bowl and drank.

The blood scorched his throat like molten fire, burning through his veins, searing down his spine. It dripped from the corners of his mouth, thick and black as ink.

Achlys leaned in, her voice now a venomous whisper.

"When she is mine, the Alpha will come for her. I will drain her life force first—shatter his heart, break his will. Then, on the full purple moon, I'll consume him too. Their deaths will unbind me from this cursed earth. I will rise, free to rule over all life."

She narrowed her eyes, her tone turning deadly.

"Do not return until then. And if you betray me... I will curse the blood in your veins. You will die screaming."

Bedwyr bowed his head and left.

He returned to Graceway, blending into the shadows, recruiting allies where he could. Most were useless—teenage rogues angry at their parents. But then, he met Frank.

CHAPTER FORTY-ONE

I groaned softly as I drifted back to consciousness.

The cold steel of the van was gone—replaced by the stale scent of dust, cheap air freshener, and something faintly sour. I blinked against the dim light, my head pounding. Disoriented, I shifted, wincing as I tried to sit up. My wrists throbbed, rubbed raw from being bound too tightly.

The big guy—Frank—sat on the edge of a worn armchair, absently flipping through motel TV channels. The screen bathed the room in a bluish flicker, filling the silence with the low hum of explosions and gunfire. I realized the noise wasn't for entertainment. It was cover. Just loud enough to mask any sounds I might make.

He noticed me stirring.

Without a word, he grabbed the syringe off the bedside table.

Panic surged through me.

"Wait—wait!" I rasped, my voice cracking from dryness. "I promise I'll behave. You don't have to inject me again."

My tongue felt like sandpaper as I licked my cracked lips, trying to moisten my mouth. "Can I please get something to drink? Maybe a snack? Or is the plan to starve me to death?" I added, sarcasm sharpening my words.

Frank narrowed his eyes, unimpressed. "Be careful. That mouth's going to get you in trouble, girl."

"My name is Gaea Angevin," I snapped, meeting his gaze. "You can stop calling me *girl*. You might be built like a truck, but I doubt you're even a day over twenty."

"I know what your name is, *girl*," he sneered. "I just don't care."

He tossed a can of cola and a small bag of chips onto the bed like I was some stray mutt. "Eat. And shut up."

"Are you going to untie my hands or feed me too?" I retorted, ripping open the chip bag with my bound fingers.

With an irritated sigh, he crossed the room and crouched beside the bed. Rough hands worked the knots free from my wrists, but he left my ankles tied.

"Is this about money?" I asked, tearing into the chips. "I have money— how much do you want?"

Frank barked out a humorless laugh. "Money? That's funny. It's not about money. Now eat. And be quiet."

"If it's not about money, then what do you want with me?" I asked cautiously, my mind racing. "Are you... animal activists or something?

Do you need my help?"

That was clearly the wrong thing to say.

"Enough," he snapped, his voice sharp and loud, echoing in the small space. "Another word, and you'll regret it."

I bit my tongue, literally.

My instincts screamed to keep pushing—to claw for information—but I forced myself into silence. I needed to stay awake, stay alert, and assess the danger. I couldn't risk another injection.

I wolfed down the salty, synthetic chips and guzzled the soda despite its sugary aftertaste. The cola coated my tongue in syrupy sweetness, the chips leaving a greasy film on my fingers. It wasn't much, but it kept the dizziness at bay.

I leaned back against the headboard, my mind already mapping escape routes again. I needed to get out. But my body betrayed me. Every limb felt like lead, my strength drained from the earlier struggle.

Rest, I told myself. Just for now. Regain strength. Watch. Wait.

With great reluctance, I let my eyes close, feigning calm while planning my next move.

CHAPTER FORTY-TWO

Cador sped down Route 88, his focus razor-sharp. The engine hummed beneath him, steady and relentless, while the scent of pine trees drifted through the open window, mixing with the cool evening air. *I can catch up to them if I drive straight through the night,* he thought grimly. *But at what cost?* He could feel the exhaustion creeping in. The mid-shift had drained too much from him—he hadn't eaten enough, hadn't rested at all.

I can't fail her.

By midnight, his body began to betray him. His vision blurred at the edges, and the muscles in his arms ached from tension. He finally veered off the road behind an abandoned diner, the lot overgrown and quiet. He ate everything he had packed, his movements mechanical and efficient. Then, without hesitation, he undressed and shifted fully into his wolf form, hoping his regenerative abilities would restore him faster.

Moonlight filtered through the shattered windows of the diner, casting long silvery streaks over his massive wolf frame as he curled up beside his truck. His thick fur rose and fell with each breath, and soon, he slipped into a deep, primal sleep.

The chill of dawn stirred him.

Around 6:00 AM, a cool breeze rustled the trees and ruffled his ears, waking him. Birds chirped somewhere in the branches above, their songs a jarring contrast to the urgency in his chest. He stretched out his limbs, testing his strength, then shifted back to his human form. After rinsing his face with bottled water, he pulled on clean clothes and got back on the road.

He kept the window down, sniffing the passing wind for any trace of her. Then, near a fading neon blue sign that read **CHRISSY'S MOTEL**, his heart stuttered.

A scent.

Gaea.

Faint but unmistakable. He slammed the brakes and pulled into the cracked parking lot at exactly 10:00 AM. Gravel crunched beneath his boots as he approached the small, run-down reception building. Inside, a flickering red "VACANT" sign buzzed above a dusty counter.

An old woman sat behind it, puffing lazily on a cigarette, her eyes fixed on a tiny television.

"Hi," he said, calm but assertive. "I'm looking for my friends. They might've stayed here last night—two men, two women?"

She squinted at him, eyes half-hidden behind curling smoke. "Only had three guests last night. Left early, 'round seven this morning. One girl, two guys. Maybe your friends drove past, love."

Cador forced a polite smile. "Thank you."

Outside, he paused and pretended to stretch. Then inhaled—deep and slow. *There you are,* he thought. *I can smell you, Gaea. I'm close.*

Don't worry, he told himself as he climbed back into the truck. *I'm coming for you.*

****

Elsewhere...

At dawn, Damean crouched inside what was left of the kennel, attempting to reinforce the broken walls with wooden planks. The room had been obliterated by Cador's violent transformation. Most of the structure was unsalvageable.

We'll need professionals to rebuild it from scratch.

But that wasn't the worst of it. The kennel was empty.

Bedwyr was gone.

And so was Gaea's car.

Damean pulled out his phone and called. "Cador—listen. Bedwyr stole Gaea's car sometime during the night. I think he's headed toward Graceway. Just thought you should know."

"Thanks, brother," Cador's voice came through tight and sharp. "Let the guys know he's waiting for me."

"Dana already called her dad," Damean added. "He dispatched a hunting party into the forest. They're sweeping the perimeter to intercept any threats. The area will be secure."

Damean hung up, concern clouding his face.

Beside him, Dana crossed her arms tightly over her chest. "I just hope Cador gets to her in time," she whispered.

CHAPTER FORTY-THREE

The big guy shoved me roughly, jolting me awake.

"Come. Let me tie your hands. If you scream, I'll jab this syringe into your neck and kill anyone who tries to help you. Got it?"

"Yes, I'll behave." I didn't want anyone else getting hurt. I obeyed and climbed into the back seat next to him.

The girl and the driver got in the front. "Aah, you trained her. Good job, Frank," the girl said, smirking.

"Shut up, Carmen," Frank snapped. "Hurry up, Johnny. We need to get back on the road."

I stared out the window, my thoughts spiraling. What was this all about? And why did it look like we were heading toward Graceway?

The van's radio blared with punk rock, each aggressive beat feeding Carmen's manic energy. The worn vinyl seats pressed against my bound arms, sticky with heat. The air reeked of stale fast food and cheap air freshener. Carmen drummed on the dashboard, singing loudly and off-key, while Johnny bobbed his head, tapping the wheel in rhythm.

I turned to Frank. His mood was as dark as the storm in my gut. He stared out the window, jaw clenched. Maybe the music grated on him, too. Then, without warning, he snapped.

"Can you turn that down? I'm trying to think."

I jumped at the sharpness in his voice.

"Geez, Franky boy," Johnny teased, glancing at him in the rearview mirror. "What's up? Aren't you excited? This is going to be awesome."

I stiffened in the corner, wrists bound tightly. Frank's ears twitched, the hair on the back of his neck standing on end. I watched him closely. He was growing more and more tense, as if hearing something no one else could.

"We're about eighteen miles from the Angevin farm," he said suddenly. "Johnny, take the back dirt road. Pass the farm—keep going until it ends. We'll walk from there."

"Yeah, sure. No problem," Johnny replied, turning the wheel casually.

Carmen twisted in her seat, eyes gleaming with cruel delight. "You're going to be part of history," she said, her voice mocking. "Achlys will take your life in front of lover boy. Then, on the purple moon, she'll break your Alpha's curse by ending her life—and finally be free."

My heart dropped. A sick churn twisted in my stomach. I could taste the bitterness of dread at the back of my throat.

The prophecy… it can't be true.

"Cador will find me," I said, forcing the words through my tight chest. "He'll stop you."

"That's exactly what we want," Carmen sneered. "His love for you will be the death of him." She threw her head back and laughed, high-pitched and manic. "Bedwyr fooled you. Shame you tried to save him."

"Bedwyr?" I asked, confused. "I've never tried to save anyone by that name."

Her laughter doubled, wild and uncontrollable. "Bedwyr is the shapeshifter—or as you knew him, the sick, frail wolf you were treating at the sanctuary. He infiltrated it to spy on you and Cador— to confirm your love. Johnny and I went in as day visitors a few days ago. We snuck into the kennel so Bedwyr could tell us *exactly* where to find you. Best plan ever!" Her wide, gleaming eyes looked almost possessed.

"That's enough," Frank growled. His voice sliced through her hysteria like a blade. "She doesn't need to know anything else."

"Why not?" Carmen shot back, defiant. "She's going to die anyway. Might as well give her a little extra fear."

Frank's eyes darkened, his voice dropping into a dangerous snarl. "If you don't shut up, I'll rip your head clean off."

Carmen paled. She turned back around, muttering, "Sure, bro. Just having some fun."

Frank's agitation only worsened as we neared the forest. Sweat poured from his skin. The heat radiating off him was unnatural.

"Guys, your friend's not well," I warned. But Frank shot me a look so chilling I snapped my mouth shut.

****

A few minutes later, Johnny pulled the van to a stop at the end of the dirt road. The forest loomed ahead—dense, dark, and whispering with unseen things. The air turned cooler. The scent of wet earth and rotting leaves curled into our lungs.

Without hesitation, Carmen jabbed the syringe into my neck.

I dropped.

"What? We can't afford to lose her," she snapped defensively.

"Frank, you're stronger. Carry her."

Frank gritted his teeth, the rage simmering just below the surface. His skin burned. His muscles twitched violently. *I've never felt this before,* he thought. *Not outside the forest. It's like I'm going to explode.*

He hoisted me over his shoulder. Limp. Unconscious. The group moved into the swamp, the weight of their twisted mission pressing down like a storm.

The terrain shifted beneath them. Hours passed. The air thickened with the stench of sulfur and decay. Insects swarmed. Mud sucked at their boots, bubbling and sticking like tar. Each step a struggle.

Frank's discomfort intensified. He clawed at his skin, breath ragged. His bones cracked. Muscles bulged. His eyes glowed an eerie yellow.

Then—he dropped me.

"What's going on, Frank? Fleas?" Carmen joked, half-heartedly.

But her smirk died fast.

They hadn't realized Bedwyr never intended for them to succeed. They were pawns. Offerings. A bloody gift for Achlys—wrapped in fear and betrayal.

From a distant cliff, Achlys watched with gleaming blue eyes. Her grin stretched wide as Frank's body contorted, overtaken by the transformation.

"Woah, big guy," Johnny stammered, backing away with raised hands. "Calm down."

They *knew* about shifters—but they'd never *seen* one shift.

Carmen bolted. No hesitation. Just fear and instinct.

Achlys clapped in delight. Her laughter echoed like bells of doom.

"Ooh, I *love* this part," she sang. "Run, rabbit, run."

Frank lunged at Johnny. The scream came too late. His jaws clamped around Johnny's hand—fingers severed cleanly. Blood filled the air.

He turned.

Carmen.

She stumbled over a rotting stump, fell face-first into the thick mud. Whimpering, she forced herself up, panting, staggering.

Too slow.

Frank landed in front of her, towering in his monstrous form. His lips curled back to reveal gleaming teeth. His eyes burned with primal hunger.

"C-come on, Franky," she stammered, backing away. "I was kidding in the van, remember? We're a team. Freedom for all, right?

Long live the Dark Queen?"

She smiled.

But the snarl that followed drowned everything else.

With terrifying speed, Frank lunged. His jaws snapped around her throat. Her scream was cut short.

Her body dropped. Unimportant. Forgotten.

He turned and charged back into the swamp.

Johnny's cries were still ringing.

CHAPTER FORTY-FOUR

Achlys descended gracefully from her perch, her bare feet silent as she moved through the mud toward Johnny. She circled him slowly, her long nails tapping rhythmically on his shoulder, like a predator toying with prey.

"What to do with a frail little thing like you?" she mused, her voice mockingly sweet. Then she leaned in close, her breath brushing his ear. **"Scream."**

"Please, don't," Johnny whimpered, clutching his mutilated hand.

"Help me. I'm bleeding—I need a hospital."

Frank emerged moments later, his hulking figure looming behind them like a beast returned to its master.

"Sit," Achlys commanded, snapping her fingers.

Without hesitation, Frank obeyed. He dropped into the mud beside her like a trained animal, motionless and alert.

"*Help me!*" she mimicked in a high, trembling voice, mocking Johnny's desperation. Her laughter rang out—sharp, cold, cruel—sending shivers crawling down Johnny's spine.

Before he could comprehend what was happening, her body began to shift.

Her bones cracked and stretched. Her limbs elongated. Her frame twisted and grew until she loomed over him—no longer a woman, but a monstrous black panther nearly ten feet tall. Muscles rippled beneath sleek fur, and her glowing blue eyes bore into him like twin flames of frost.

"No… no, please!" Johnny sobbed, scrambling backward through the mud, dragging his broken body.

But it was useless.

With one swift motion, Achlys pounced, pinning him down. His screams were short-lived. She opened her massive jaws and swallowed him whole.

Silence fell.

She licked her lips, savoring the final trace of him on her tongue. Then her body shrank and cracked back into her human form. Calm and composed, she dusted her hands off as though she'd just cleaned up a meal.

She turned to Frank, who remained seated in obedient stillness.

Achlys lifted Gaea's limp form with supernatural ease, draping her over Frank's broad back before climbing up herself like a rider on a war beast.

"Go, Frank," she ordered, jabbing her heel into his ribs. "Head north. There's a cave. The others are waiting."

Frank obeyed at once, plodding through the swamp with heavy, wet footsteps, vanishing into the shadows like a specter of death.

Achlys paused, glancing back across the dark forest.

Her eyes narrowed. She inhaled deeply. "The Alpha comes," she whispered. "I feel her rage vibrating through the trees."

She turned back toward the cave, a cruel smile curling her lips.

"Prepare yourself, Frank. The final act is about to begin."

CHAPTER FORTY-FIVE

Cador arrived at the Angevin farm just as the sun dipped below the horizon, painting the fields in deep hues of amber and violet. The fading light cast long shadows over the rolling land, the air thick with tension and the scent of dusk.

Seven of the strongest pack warriors awaited him near the barn, their towering forms a reassuring sight against the encroaching dark.

"Good evening, Your Grace. Welcome back," Aiden greeted, clasping his hand in a firm shake before pulling him into a quick embrace. His voice held both respect and relief. "We've been waiting. But the party you mentioned never passed by us. They must have taken a different route."

"It's good to see you all again," Cador replied, his tone steady but edged with urgency. "There's an old dirt road at the far edge of the southern fields. It leads straight into the swamp—they would've used it to avoid detection."

Aiden nodded. "Makes sense."

"Achlys won't kill Gaea tonight," Cador continued, his gaze sweeping the darkening horizon. "She's waiting for me. She wants me to feel it—to see her take Gaea's life with my own eyes." He inhaled slowly. "We'll camp here for the night. I need to replenish my strength. Tomorrow… will demand all of it."

Without hesitation, Lugh and Oisín disappeared into the woods to hunt. They returned an hour later with a massive boar, its bulk barely manageable between them. The warriors set to work swiftly, lighting a fire and preparing the meat. The scent of sizzling pork and wild rosemary mingled with smoke, briefly easing the weight of what was to come.

The warriors ate in near silence, the fire crackling at their feet. Their minds were already in the battle to come.

When the meal was done, Cador stood and addressed the group, his presence commanding even in the low firelight.

"Shift into your wolf forms tonight. It will conserve your energy for tomorrow. Rest well."

The men nodded solemnly before shifting. The field was soon filled with hulking wolves, their forms curling into the earth beneath the moonlight. Cador remained human for a while longer, his golden eyes scanning the stars above, his thoughts consumed by one name.

Gaea.

****

The first rays of dawn pierced the mist. Cador was already awake.

I'm not far from you, my love, he thought, nose lifted to the breeze.

The pack stirred with the rising light. By 9 a.m., they were assembled and ready to move.

In his sleek wolf form, Cador addressed the warriors through the telepathic bond, his thoughts sharp and clear.

"Dylan. Colin. Stay here. If Bedwyr circles back this way, intercept him. He's infected with Achlys's blood. He's not as strong as she is, but still dangerous. It might take both of you."

The two wolves dipped their heads, expressions grim.

"Aiden. Oisín. Lugh. Bran. Owen—you're with me," Cador continued. **"Achlys is using another omega to help guard Gaea. There were two humans with them as well, though she has no real use for them. They might interfere."**

With a nod, the group took off, running swift and silent through the tall grass. Cador led them, his nose trained on the faint trace of Gaea's scent, drifting south like a ghost on the wind.

Despite the urgency, he conserved his strength. He hadn't shifted into his full Alpha form—and he wouldn't unless absolutely necessary. That power… was still a part of him he didn't fully trust.

They traveled quickly, the air growing heavier with every mile. Then came the stench—coppery, thick, unmistakable.

They stumbled upon a grisly sight.

A woman's dismembered corpse lay sprawled in the underbrush, limbs mangled as if torn apart for amusement. Her blood soaked the earth.

The pack froze, hackles raised.

Cador stepped forward, rage flaring in his golden eyes.

"This wasn't a warning," he growled through the bond. **"This was done for sport. Achlys."**

They pressed onward, the mood darker, the tension a taut string ready to snap. The forest thickened, and the air turned acrid. The smell of sulfur grew stronger. Insects buzzed like a chorus of death.

They reached the cave system on the north side by midday.

The entrance yawned before them—dark, wet, and reeking of decay. Shadows moved unnaturally inside, as if the cave breathed.

Cador stepped forward, eyes narrowing.

"Stay alert," he commanded. **"She's here. And so is Achlys."**

CHAPTER FORTY-SIX

Bedwyr drove relentlessly through the night, his eyes fixed and unwavering on the road ahead. By the time the first light of dawn crept over the horizon, he had reached the edge of town. Without hesitation, he veered off the main road and drove Gaea's car into a ditch, concealing it behind a dense wall of brambles and bushes.

It was early Friday morning. Despite the hours on the road, he felt no fatigue. Achlys' blood surged through his veins, invigorating him with unnatural strength. It fed on her excitement—boundless, dark, and euphoric.

He stepped into the underbrush and stripped off his clothes. The shift came fast, brutal. His bones cracked and twisted, limbs bending unnaturally as his body contorted into wolf form. Where once his coat had been sleek and shining, it was now patchy, rough—blemished by the curse Achlys had gifted him.

When it ended, his form radiated raw strength, but his appearance told the truth: he was a creature tainted, altered. A vessel of borrowed power.

Without pause, he darted into the forest from the north, weaving through trees with relentless speed. He knew how the pack operated—some would remain in the village, others would guard the Angevin farm, and Cador would lead the strongest south.

But Bedwyr had one purpose. **Reach Achlys. Stand by her. See it through.**

I felt his power that night, he thought as he ran, paws thundering against the forest floor. *When they took Gaea, and he mid-shifted… we underestimated him. Cador is stronger than I imagined. She'll need me.*

He ran harder, driven by more than duty—by obsession, by devotion, by the sickening promise of victory. For four hours he pushed forward, until at last the earth grew hot beneath his feet, and the stench of sulfur thickened the air.

The caves loomed ahead, dark and suffocating. He shifted back into human form, his body folding in on itself with painful cracks. Staggering, he made his way into the shadowed maw of the cave.

"Did you miss me, my queen?" he rasped, voice rough from exertion but laced with reverence.

From the depths of the cave, she emerged.

Achlys.

She stepped into the low light, her human form somehow more terrifying than her monstrous one. Tall, statuesque, eyes like shattered ice. Her lips curled into a cruel smile as she approached.

"I must say, Bedwyr… I'm impressed," she purred, circling him like a panther. "Never in my wildest dreams did I think my victory would come at the hands of a beta lone wolf."

Her fingers trailed across his shoulders, slow and deliberate.

"You've earned your place. Today, I take the girl's life force. And tomorrow night—" her voice rose, giddy with malice, "the defeated Alpha's. At last, the curse will be broken. And I… will be free."

Bedwyr shifted slightly, tension coiling in his shoulders. "My queen," he said, the title catching in his throat, "I must warn you. Cador is… more powerful than we believed. That night—when he mid-shifted— his energy, his restraint… even in fury, he held back. He didn't go full size. Please, do not underestimate him."

Achlys laughed, the sound echoing through the cavern like the shriek of a banshee. Cold. Mocking.

"They all think they're powerful," she sneered. "Until they step onto *my* battlefield. Amena thought the same. I took her. I took most of her children. Cador will fall like the rest."

She stepped closer, her breath brushing his cheek.

"I've gifted your rejected brethren with some of my blood. They'll help in the battle to come. Together, we'll crush him. You'll see."

Just then, a faint sound echoed through the cave—movement.

Both froze.

Achlys turned her head slowly toward the noise, her smile fading. The scent of something familiar—too familiar—drifted in.

Cador.

CHAPTER FORTY-SEVEN

I slowly regained consciousness, my movements sluggish but deliberate as I sat upright. My head felt... clear. Unnaturally clear, as if a veil had been lifted from my mind. The air was thick with the stench of damp cave walls and rot, but it was the presence looming in front of me that demanded my attention—Frank, in wolf form, his rancid breath curling in the air like poison.

Yet... I wasn't afraid anymore.

Memories, long buried and locked away, surged back all at once—raw and real. Each one painted in sharp detail. Niamh had been right. Returning to the forest had awakened something.

And I finally understood.

"It was you," I said, my voice stronger than I expected—sharp enough to slice through the silence. "You psychotic, power-hungry lunatic." I stared directly at Achlys, the words spilling out like venom. "You're the one who took my parents that night in the woods. But you left me. Why?"

Achlys turned to me, her expression unreadable at first, then slowly curled into a knowing smirk.

"Silly little girl... why do you think?" she purred. "For *this*. I cannot break the curse without your love for the Alpha. I needed you to grow, to *feel*, to fulfill your destiny."

I shook my head, still stunned. "But how did you know we'd ever meet? I moved so far away."

"It didn't matter if you ran to the ends of the earth," she said, smugness dripping from every word. "You were *bound* to him centuries ago. Nothing could change that. I saw it that very morning after I took your parents—he imprinted on you instantly, even if neither of you realized it. You weren't afraid of him. You followed him without question. That was all the proof I needed."

"I remember..." I whispered, a tremor in my voice—not from fear, but from something deeper. My heart surged with a fierce, all-consuming love for Cador. That moment in the woods all those years ago... it *was* real.

I lifted my chin, defiance burning in my chest. "He will stop you," I said, a smirk tugging at my lips. "His power isn't just in his strength—it's in his heart. And it's pure. He cares."

Achlys clicked her tongue and shook her head mockingly. "Tsk, tsk. Poor, naïve little girl. Cormac Angevin thought the same thing, long ago. His 'pure heart' couldn't save him. He wasn't willing to kill me, so he banished me instead. And look where that got him."

My glare sharpened. "Well, I won't hold it against Cador if he rips your head off."

And then—clear and unmistakable—his voice echoed inside my mind, warm and steady:

"Aw, thanks, love. That's good news, because I intend to do just that."

I spun around, heart leaping into my throat. At the mouth of the cave stood a pack of wolves—fierce, glowing, unstoppable. But all I could see were his eyes. Cador. His amber gaze blazed like twin fires, locking onto mine.

Relief poured through me like sunlight breaking through storm clouds.

Achlys snarled, cutting the moment short. "It's not time yet," she hissed.

Before I could react, she seized me and hurled me onto Frank's back. I barely managed to hold on as the massive wolf lurched forward. Achlys kicked him in the ribs. "Go!"

Frank barreled deeper into the cave, with Bedwyr close behind, his movements unsteady and frantic.

At the entrance, Cador inhaled sharply, but the air was thick with sulfur, drowning out my scent. Still, he focused, mind racing.

She's leading us into a trap, he said telepathically, his tone grim. **This cave tunnels north—near the stream where Gaea's parents were taken. That's where she needs to complete the ritual. That's where she'll try to break the curse.**

He turned to the others. **We'll split. Circle around. Trap her the other side.**

Without hesitation, the pack dispersed, melting into the forest like smoke on the wind. They ran with unrelenting purpose, hearts pounding in unison.

They all knew.

The final battle had begun.

CHAPTER FORTY-EIGHT

Cador had been right.

Achlys had assembled a pack of ten omega lone wolves, each one corrupted and strengthened by her blood. Twisted by her magic, they now possessed power that rivaled even betas. No longer fully human or wolf, these abominations stood in mid-shift—monstrous hybrids with the brute strength of wolves and the dexterity of men. It was a form only true Alphas could reach on their own.

But Cador's strength was beyond compare. Even with her blood amplifying their abilities, they were no match for him.

They weren't meant to be.

These wolves were distractions—flesh-and-blood obstacles designed to stall his warriors, to isolate him. Achlys wanted him alone. She needed him to watch. To witness Gaea's death. To break under the weight of helplessness and grief. Only then would he be vulnerable enough to surrender—so she could take his life beneath the full purple moon and finally break her ancient curse.

Cador threw his head back and howled, the sound reverberating across the forest like a thunderclap. It echoed for miles—reaching even as far as Graceway.

Dylan and Colin, stationed near the village, heard the call. Without hesitation, they broke into a sprint, racing toward him. At full speed, they'd reach the battlefield in under an hour.

Meanwhile, deeper in the woods, Achlys had bound Gaea to a thick oak, using twine woven from enchanted forest shrubs. She crouched beside her, talon-like fingernails dragging slowly across Gaea's skin—slicing shallow wounds that bled freely.

Red rivulets trickled to the earth.

It wasn't just torture. It was bait.

The scent of Gaea's blood, thick and sweet, filled the air—an invisible snare meant to pierce Cador's instincts, to cloud his judgment. Rage. Desperation. Confusion. Achlys wanted all of it.

And still, Gaea didn't scream.

Achlys stood and turned away, her attention shifting to the chaos unraveling around her. Wolves clashed in brutal combat—flesh tearing, bones snapping, the forest floor soaked in crimson. She drank in the carnage, her lips curled in delight, her eyes wild with elation.

The scent of blood. The sound of agony.

This was ecstasy.

And for a brief, fatal moment—**she forgot Gaea.**

CHAPTER FORTY-NINE

Blood dripped steadily from my wrists, seeping into the bark where Achlys had tied me to the ancient oak. The wounds stung, but something strange—*miraculous*—began to happen.

The twine binding my hands began to loosen on its own.

I blinked through the pain. The ground beneath me shifted, almost imperceptibly, as if lifting to support me. The wind whispered through the trees, and I swear—I swear—a branch brushed against my shoulder, nudging me gently. Urging me to move.

The forest... was helping me.

My scent drifted with the breeze, carried away from the battlefield. Away from Achlys.

I didn't hesitate.

I slipped free and bolted, my bare feet making no sound on the soft forest floor. The earth cushioned my every step, guiding me like an unseen hand. It felt like Ichika herself was shielding me, pushing me toward safety.

I knew exactly where I needed to go.

The cave.

The one Cador had taken me to that night—when everything had changed. Niamh had told me long ago that it was sacred, protected by the forest's old magic. I trusted that he would find me there.

And I believed, with everything in me, that I would be safe.

****

Achlys didn't notice until it was too late.

"She's *gone!*" she shrieked, her voice ripping through the forest like a banshee's wail. Her fury crackled in the air, raw and electric.

At that moment, Dylan and Colin arrived, their eyes immediately locking onto the chaos of the battlefield.

"Go!" they shouted to Cador. "Find Gaea—we've got this!"

Cador didn't hesitate.

He heard Achlys's cry and knew exactly what it meant. He took off, faster than he'd ever moved before. Trees whipped past him, his muscles burning, but his focus never wavered.

****

"Slow him down!" Achlys barked at Bedwyr, her expression fierce and unrelenting.

"But he'll kill me," Bedwyr stammered, trembling in his half-shifted form.

"I don't care," she snarled, her hand clenching into a fist.

Bedwyr gasped, clutching his chest as if invisible claws were crushing his heart.

"You swore your life to me," she hissed. "Now *prove it.*"

And then she was gone, vanishing into the trees as she picked up Gaea's scent again.

****

Cador found Bedwyr minutes later, standing alone in the clearing, twisted and monstrous in his corrupted mid-shift form. The hybrid shape was grotesque—limbs too long, spine arched unnaturally, eyes glowing with something far from human.

"I don't have time for games, Bedwyr," Cador growled, his voice deepening as he rose into full shift. His massive frame radiated raw, ancient power, eyes burning gold.

Bedwyr sneered. "Achlys will take you down."

Cador responded with a guttural snarl and lunged.

The battle was over in seconds.

He sank his teeth deep into Bedwyr's throat, his powerful jaws crunching through bone. A single twist. A final snap.

Cador released the body, spitting out the foul taste. His mind was already on Gaea.

He turned and ran.

Faster.

The forest became a blur, trees bending to let him pass, his heart hammering like war drums.

He had to reach her—*before Achlys did.*

CHAPTER FIFTY

"I know you're here somewhere, little girl," Achlys hissed, her voice slithering through the trees like a venomous serpent.

I crouched low behind a thick tree trunk, holding my breath. I could hear her footsteps as she prowled through the forest.

"You're clever," she sneered, her tone laced with admiration and disdain. "I see you've learned to use nature—just like your great ancestor Cormac."

The truth was, I had no idea *how* I was doing it. I only knew I needed to hide. And somehow, the forest responded to that need. The leaves shifted to shield me, shadows deepened around me, and even the wind played its part—carrying my scent away from her piercing blue eyes as they scanned the underbrush.

"I never told anyone this," Achlys murmured, her voice softening to something almost human, almost wistful. "But I *loved* Cormac. And for a time, I believed he loved me, too. But his love made him weak. He refused to use his power to set me free from Ichika."

Her voice grew bitter. "He wanted to stay here and *save lives*—while I wanted to *rule* them. And then he and my sister, Amena, made their little pact. They couldn't bring themselves to kill me, so they banished me to the farthest edge of the forest. Alone. Forever. That's what love gets you." Her tone turned icy. "Love is a sickness, not a power. And it won't save you, little girl."

I didn't realize she had circled the tree until it was too late. Her icy hand clamped down on my wrist, yanking me to my feet. Her grip was like iron, her smirk triumphant as her cold eyes met mine.

But then—*a low growl rumbled through the forest.*

Cador had arrived.

Achlys spun around, dragging me in front of her like a shield. I could feel her hesitation. Cador was shifting before our eyes.

And what a sight he was.

Even Achlys looked momentarily stunned as she watched his transformation. I couldn't help the way my breath hitched, my eyes wide with awe and relief.

He rose to his full height, standing upright on powerful hind legs. His form was a breathtaking fusion of man and beast—raw strength and unearthly grace. His paws thickened, his torso widened, and his shoulders tripled in size. Sharp claws gleamed at the end of muscular forearms. His ears sharpened into perfect points, and his amber eyes glowed like wildfire. Every part of him radiated dominance, purpose, and fury.

Achlys flinched—and then, snarled.

She hurled me to the ground, slamming me against a nearby tree. Pain exploded across my back, but I was conscious.

"Stay there!" she barked. "I'll deal with you shortly."

****

She turned back to Cador, her lips curling into a cruel smile.

"Well, well, Alpha. Looks like we have ourselves a standoff." Her voice dripped with venom. "No matter. I'll hurt you *just enough* to keep you alive—so you can watch her die. Then I'll drag you to my cave and end you beneath the purple full moon tomorrow night."

Cador's voice was low and steady, his fury unmistakable. "I'm sick of hearing about the 'all-powerful Achlys.' All I see is a lonely witch using broken men to do her dirty work. Stop hiding. Show me what you *really* are."

Achlys laughed—a jagged, cruel sound. "Very well, little Alpha."

Her body began to shift—but her transformation was not like Cador's. It was harsh, strained, grotesque.

She grew into a towering, panther-like beast nearly ten feet tall. Black fur covered her warped form, her claws elongated, her icy blue eyes glowing with rage. But there was no grace in her. No balance. She was power without harmony. A twisted mockery of what Cador had become.

Then they collided.

The earth trembled with the force of their blows. Claws slashed through air. Teeth gnashed. The air crackled with energy as the two monsters fought with everything they had.

Achlys struck first, her claws tearing across Cador's chest, blood splattering the forest floor. Cador roared and retaliated, clamping his jaws around her shoulder and ripping free a chunk of flesh. She screamed, lashing out and clawing deep into his back, forcing him to his knees.

She turned toward me, triumphant. "Now it's your turn," she snarled, raising her claws to strike.

But her moment of victory shattered.

Cador rose.

With a final, furious surge of power, he sprang forward. His muscles coiled, his claws extended. He reached her before she could react.

And with one devastating motion—he tore the top half of her head clean off.

The forest fell still.

Achlys's body dropped to the earth with a sickening thud, her blood soaking into the soil.

Cador stood over her, chest heaving, his sides streaked with blood. He was shaking—wounded, exhausted, but alive. He looked at me, and the intensity in his eyes softened.

It wasn't pride that filled him. It was *relief*.

He had saved me.

CHAPTER FIFTY-ONE

The few lone wolves who had remained under Achlys's influence scattered into the forest, free now—but afraid. They knew Cador was still alive, and none dared stay long enough to see what vengeance he might bring. Frank, too, vanished into the trees without a trace.

The wolves who had fought the omegas came to find us. Cador had reverted to his human form, completely drained, his head resting in my lap. I held him close, pressing down on the wound in his shoulder, tears slipping silently down my cheeks.

"Please be okay," I whispered.

One of the wolves approached. "Hi, I'm Aiden," he said gently. "We'll take him back to our village. He needs food and rest."

Carefully, he shifted into his wolf form, then picked Cador up in his mouth and placed him gently on another wolf's back.

"Come," Aiden urged. "Grab my mane and climb on. You look like you could use a warm bath and a good meal."

"Please—no rabbit," I muttered, managing a laugh. "The last time a pack made me a meal, it... lacked flavor."

A ripple of laughter echoed through the wolves. They'd clearly heard the tale of the human girl who couldn't stomach Milak's cooking.

It was nearly midnight.

For the first time in what felt like forever, the villagers of Ichika were finally free.

****

We reached the village not long after. Aiden knelt to let me slide off his back. I was immediately struck by the warmth and light of the place. A massive bonfire burned in the center of the village, casting golden shadows across houses that looked more like cozy cabins than primitive dwellings. They reminded me of the sanctuary bungalows in Wave Crest—complete with solar panels, gravel paths, and neatly carved wooden doors. Streetlights lined the roads. A tractor rumbled softly in the distance.

"I feel ridiculous now," I murmured. "I pictured something far more primitive... Not a beautiful, developed place like this."

Aiden chuckled. "We're not like the cities. No TVs, and only phones for emergencies. We live more like a homestead community. We've survived this way for generations. We go into town, mingle with the locals, take our crops to the markets... no one ever suspects."

"They still do that?" I asked, surprised.

"Every Saturday. Like clockwork," he said with a grin. "Come, I'll take you to Cador's home. We'll lay him in bed, and someone will tend to his wounds."

"No need. I'll look after him myself. But—do you think I could borrow some clean clothes? I've been thrown around, dropped in mud, and smacked into a tree... I think half the forest is still clinging to me." I giggled.

"Absolutely. We'll bring some over," he promised.

Cador's house was three times the size of his Wave Crest cabin—built for a family, not just one man. Inside, they carried him to the main bedroom and laid him down gently.

Moments later, Milak and Bridget entered.

"Hi, I'm Bridget, and this is—"

"Milak," I said with a smile. "We met years ago."

His face lit up. "I see your memory has returned."

"Among other things," I said with a nervous laugh.

Bridget stepped forward, carrying folded clothes. "These are from Dana's closet. They should fit you. We'll bring food and drink, and warm water is already running for a bath. I'll send someone with herbs to clean your and Cador's wounds."

"Thank you," I said softly.

A young girl arrived not long after, balancing a basket of bread, cheese, fruits, meaty stew, and freshly squeezed juice. In her other hand was a small pouch filled with herbal wraps and salves. I thanked her warmly and sent her on her way.

I lit the copper taps and ran a hot bath, tossing in dried yarrow and chamomile to infuse the water with healing warmth. The steam was already rising when I returned to the room to check on Cador.

He was sitting up, eyes groggy but alert.

"Hey, you," I whispered. "How are you feeling?"

"Like a panther ran me over," he groaned with a half-laugh, clutching his ribs. "Are you going to take a bath?"

"Yes. And by the smell of things… so are you."

"That sounded suspiciously like an invitation," he teased.

I took his hand with a grin. "Come on. After everything I saw today, there's nothing left to surprise me."

I helped him out of bed and into the bathroom. He moved slowly, wincing with each step, but determined. Out of respect, he kept his eyes closed while I undressed and slipped into the water.

He followed, lowering himself in beside me. We didn't speak much.

The warm water wrapped around us like a blanket, washing away days of pain, blood, and fear.

For now, there was no battle. No prophecy. No curses.

Only the soothing silence.

And each other.

CHAPTER FIFTY-TWO

Early the next morning, I sat up straight in bed. I felt refreshed and rested, the weight of the past few days lifted. I was wearing one of Cador's oversized T-shirts—it smelled like him, like pine and something wild.

"What's wrong, love?" Cador murmured, brushing his fingers gently up my spine.

"I was just thinking…" I paused. "I love Wave Crest, but I love you more. You said the sanctuary there is just your holiday home. What if we opened one here—on my family's farm?"

He blinked, listening intently.

"Dana and Damean can manage the Wave Crest sanctuary. You and I could stay here and help everyone. Graceway needs a vet. I could open a wildlife practice and help the locals with their livestock, like my father did. I want to be near you. Near our people. If that's what you want too?"

Cador grabbed me and pulled me against him, his eyes searching mine. "I love that idea. You would do that... for me?"

I smiled. "Not just for you. For us. I only have my practical exams left next month, then I'm done. Which means while I'm there, I can pack up, sell my house, and move everything to the farm. Best of both worlds."

"And Jerry? You can't leave him behind."

"Of course not. We'll bring him here. He'll love it—and if he gets lost in the forest, the kids will probably find him and bring him back. As long as he has his Jello, he'll be just fine." I giggled.

Cador leaned in, placing a long, warm kiss on my lips before sitting up. "Coffee?"

"Coffee sounds amazing. You stay—I'll make us a cup," I said, sliding out of bed.

A few minutes later, I felt him behind me, warm and solid, his lips brushing my neck as his hand traced up my thigh.

"You know," he whispered into my ear, "the prophecy says we need to be married under the purple full moon."

Goosebumps spread across my skin. I felt him press closer. My knees went weak.

"Please say yes?"

I turned to face him. "Are you asking me to marry you?"

He scooped me up onto the kitchen counter, eye level now, his gaze steady and reverent.

"We've been through more than most couples ever could. I'm asking you now—marry me tonight, under the purple full moon, as we were always meant to."

My heart overflowed. Joy, fierce and pure, flooded my chest.

"Yes," I whispered. "I'd go to the ends of the earth for you."

He lifted me off the counter, wrapping my legs around his waist and kissing me deeply. His energy passed through me like a current— wild, overwhelming, perfect.

He pulled back and gently set me down.

"Then it's settled. Tonight, we celebrate. Tonight, we become one."

Still in his boxer shorts, Cador bolted out the door, shouting into the early morning:

"She said yes! Bake your best bread! Take a cow and a sheep— prepare it all for tonight! We need a dress! A wedding cake! It's a feast!"

Then he came back in, beaming.

"Thank you for making me whole. I've loved you since the first day I saw you," he said softly, kissing me again.

****

It was a flurry of joyful chaos. Young and old came to help. One woman wove flowers into my hair. Another adjusted Niamh's old wedding dress to fit me. By dusk, everything was ready.

The bonfire burned brightly in the center of the village, casting a golden glow across the gathering. The scent of roasted meats and wildflowers filled the air. Laughter and music danced in the wind.

Milak arrived to fetch me. He took my arm and guided me through the village as people sang and tossed white flowers at my feet. He led me into the assembly hall, a large barn-like structure transformed with lights and fabric and garlands of white blooms.

On one side stood a table longer than anything I'd ever seen, covered in cream linens and runners, decorated with bouquets of soft white flowers.

Villagers lined up in two rows, forming an aisle.

Milak walked me down, then left me at the altar—where Cador stood waiting, his eyes never leaving mine.

The officiant had us repeat simple vows. Promises of eternal love. Of loyalty. Of choosing one another again and again.

Then Cador leaned in and kissed me, sealing our union.

Cheers and song erupted from the crowd.

Hand in hand, we walked back out toward the feast. Villagers played joyful music, and a young girl's ethereal voice lifted above the instruments, casting a spell over us all.

Oisín, Lugh, Aiden, and Colin brought in a large wooden table as the women laid out platters of cheese, fruits, rustic breads, and roasted vegetables. Young men carried in trays of roasted meats—rich, savory scents that made my stomach rumble.

Cador took his seat at the head of the table, I at his right. He stood and raised his glass.

"I want to thank my new wife," he said, voice strong and full. "Thank you for loving me, even after seeing my true form. Thank you for choosing to leave your home behind to be here with me. To all my brothers who fought bravely yesterday—thank you. And to the women who helped Gaea prepare, thank you."

He grinned. "Now—let's eat!"

The crowd erupted in cheers.

The elders and families with small children were served first. Cador and I waited, as tradition dictated. The alpha and his mate always served last.

It was a night to remember. We laughed, we danced, we celebrated. And when no one noticed, we slipped away.

****

Cador carried me back to the house, cradling me as if I weighed nothing. The village women had decorated our bedroom—white petals scattered over the floor, gauzy linen draped from the four-poster bed, a fire crackling in the hearth. On the dresser sat chilled champagne and a tray of fruits.

He set me gently on the floor, taking my chin in his hand and gazing into my eyes.

"I love you with all my heart, Mrs. Whelan," he whispered.

"And I love you, Mr. Whelan."

He pulled the pins from my hair, letting it tumble freely down my back. His gaze never wavered. Slowly, he slid the dress from my shoulders until it pooled at my feet. He placed his hand at the small of my back, drawing me closer.

A shiver of anticipation ran through me. This was it—the night we'd waited for. No more longing. No more barriers.

He kissed me, unhurried and deep, as we made our way to the bed, shedding the remnants of the outside world.

What we shared that night was more than passion.

It was destiny.

This   was   what   true   love   felt   like.

EPILOGUE

As the fires of celebration dwindled and quiet settled over the village of Ichicka, Gaea and Cador held each other close, knowing that peace, though hard-won, was only the beginning.

Their family was growing, and with it, new challenges awaited.

Their four children—Rauol, the quiet and wild firstborn with a heart of gold destined to one day lead; the twins Cai and Percy, fierce shifters bound by blood and loyalty; and Drustan, their youngest, the only human among them— would soon face a world shadowed by a new threat.

When the family moved away from Ichicka, a savage beast

stalked the forest, claiming the lives of villagers and townfolk who dared to camp beneath its canopy. Its dark presence lingered, a silent danger still hunting in the wild.

Far from the pack's turmoil, Niva, daughter of Aiden and Cyna, lived a life apart—haunted by the loss of her father to the beast and driven by dreams of design and speed at Wave Crest University. Yet beneath her fierce independence lay a secret, buried deep and hidden from her until the day her nineteenth birthday revealed a truth recorded only in the pages of Cormac's diary.

That truth would shatter her world and bind her fate to Rauol's in ways neither could imagine.

As Rauol reaches out across the chaos to earn her trust, their lives are set on a collision course — one fraught with betrayal, ancient dangers, and the wild beast that threatens them all.

Their story is only just beginning.